Alfred W. Cole

Reminiscences of My Life and of the Cape Bench and Bar

Alfred W. Cole

Reminiscences of My Life and of the Cape Bench and Bar

ISBN/EAN: 9783337720216

Printed in Europe, USA, Canada, Australia, Japan

Cover: Foto ©Andreas Hilbeck / pixelio.de

More available books at **www.hansebooks.com**

REMINISCENCES OF MY LIFE

AND OF

THE CAPE BENCH AND BAR.

BY

THE HON. MR. JUSTICE COLE,

RETIRED JUDGE OF THE SUPREME COURT OF THE CAPE COLONY.

J. C. JUTA AND CO.,

CAPE TOWN | PORT ELIZABETH

JOHANNESBURG.

1896.

To my Daughter,

MRS. H. TOWNLEY WRIGHT,

WHO HAS BEEN MY SOLE AMANUENSIS
IN THE WRITING OF THIS WORK, I NOW INSCRIBE IT, WITH
SINCERE AFFECTION AND GRATITUDE.

THE AUTHOR.

PREFACE.

IN these days when Reminiscences are dealt forth so
freely to the Public, it may seem presumption on my
part to obtrude my own; but as the people I have
been dealing with, and the scenes in which they act,
differ so widely from those, for instance, of the late
Mr. Serjeant Ballantyne and of the late Mr. Montague
Williams, Q.C., I venture to hope that I may secure
a few readers not only in this Colony but in
England.

Anacreon says :—

> "I fain would sound th' Atreides' praise,
> To Cadmus too my song would raise,
> But that my harp denies its tone
> To any theme save Love alone."

As least, so I translate his words.   Now I do not
possess a harp, and could not play on it if I did, but
I have some fear that the steel pen which does duty
for it with me may in the following pages have
harped too much on one theme—myself.   I am sorry
for this, but I cannot help it.   But I think it must
be almost impossible to write one's personal reminiscences without being egotistical.

Madame de Goncourt tells us that it is difficult to
avoid giving offence when writing personalities, and

she adds : " *Surtout quand on a des affaires avec les gens de la Cour.*" The French authoress' "*gens*" and her "*Cour*" differ greatly from the people I have endeavoured to sketch, or the court or courts in which they mostly play their parts, but her saying applies to all alike. I have endeavoured, as far as possible, to avoid offensive personalities, bearing in mind Othello's injunction to "nothing extenuate or set down in malice," especially as regards persons still living. I hope I have offended no one, but if I should find that I have unwittingly done so, my repentance will be sincere and my apologies ungrudged.

One word more. The whole of this book, from first page to last, has been composed without any reference to diary, memoranda, or note-book—I have none. I have had to rely entirely on my own memory, but I trust it will be found that I have not made many mistakes in regard to events, times, places, or persons.

A. W. C.

WYNBERG,
    NEAR CAPE TOWN.
        May, 1896.

CONTENTS.

REMINISCENCES OF MY LIFE

CAPE BENCH AND BAR.

CHAPTER I.

Early Life—False Start—Called to Bar—Benchers—Dickens—
Thackeray—Cruikshank.

WHEN and where I was born can have but little
interest to the reader, but I may state briefly that I
first saw the light in the year 1823, at what was then
a beautiful suburb of London, but which has since
been absorbed into the jaws of the great city, and
spoilt by being covered by pastry-cook architecture
in the shape of stuccoed villas. I was educated
partly at the London University and partly at a
private school, where I imbibed a sincere love for
cricket and classics. Of course I attended to my
mathematics also, but they did not gain much of
my affection. Which is the better mental training?
I can only reply that I think ferreting out the meaning of a Greek chorus and analysing its language is
quite as good intellectual exercise as solving tough
mathematical problems. "But *cui bono?*" asks the
reader—"what is the use of your classics?" I
answer, "They are very useful in my profession;

B

and now in my old age, when my weakness of sight almost prevents me from reading, I find great pleasure in recalling favourite passages from the Latin, and sometimes the Greek poets, and making mental translations of them into English verse. I doubt whether conic sections or the differential calculus would afford me as much consolation."

My first start in life after the education days were over (are they ever over ?) was to enter the office of an uncle of mine, a London solicitor of large and somewhat exclusive practice. He had most of the colleges of the University of Cambridge as his clients, and he would have nothing to do with " criminal," " bankruptcy," or " insolvent cases." The routine of an attorney's office, however, did not suit my taste, and my uncle and I agreed to part company. It was some time before my future career was decided on; but eventually I joined the Middle Temple to keep my terms for the Bar.

Among my fellow "students" were the late Charles Dickens and the late William Makepeace Thackeray. Dickens, although he kept more than the requisite number of terms, never chose to be called to the Bar; but Thackeray, on the contrary, after the usual probation, became a barrister-at-law. On a man's " call-day " it is usual for him to invite a few of the most intimate of his friends among the students to dine with him, he providing the wine for the occasion. Either Thackeray did not know of this custom, or did not care enough for any of the students to ask them to join him; so he sat down to dinner in the midst of strangers only. *Vis-à-vis* to him sat the cheekiest young gentleman I ever

knew, and whom I have always regarded as the
original of Thackeray's Foker. Thackeray observed
the absence of wine, the usual bottle supplied to
each mess of four being wanting.

" There's no wine," he observed.

" No," replied Foker; " it's your ' call-day,' and
you're expected to provide it."

" Oh, I beg pardon ! " replied Thackeray. " I did
not know that. What wine shall it be ? "

" I should say champagne," suggested Foker; and
in a few minutes two bottles stood on the table.

Foker then tried to draw cut the great man in
conversation; but Thackeray was very reticent except
among his intimate friends, when he was a most
genial and jovial companion. I am afraid Foker
could derive no satisfaction from his meeting except
the honour of having dined with him.

After his admission to the Bar, Thackeray took
chambers in the Temple, but steadfastly refused all
briefs brought to him, having neither the inclination,
nor perhaps the qualification, for practising his profession. He was quite right; and it would have been
a great pity if he had wasted in the Law Courts the
splendid qualities which made him, in my opinion,
the greatest of modern novelists.

Amongst the benchers of our Inn were Sir Alexander
Cockburn, the Attorney-General, and Sir Richard
Bethell, the Solicitor-General : the former was very
popular among the students on account of his well-
known *bonhomie*, but Bethell was looked at somewhat askance, being justly credited with a sarcastic
and bitter tongue. Cockburn was undoubtedly the
greatest orator of the English Bar. Bethell had no

pretensions to what is commonly called. oratory, but
I never listened to a more lucid or persuasive speaker.
There was also among the benchers a little, old,
hunchbacked Baronet, who was also popular amongst
the students, but from a different cause.   The
students had some funny stories to tell about him ;
but, as *virginibus puerisque canto* (or rather *scribo*),
I shall refrain from telling any of them.   It is sufficient to say that the old gentleman's morals were
not supposed to be quite as strait-laced as those of
his namesake, the tutor of Sandford and Merton.

In due time I was also called to the Bar.   As a
matter of course I took chambers, and, equally as a
matter of course, waited in vain for the rush of briefs
which did not come, and had to be contented with
the few driblets that did.   So I made a dash for
literature, and my first ' Legend in Verse,' *à la*
Ingoldsby, was warmly welcomed by the celebrated
publisher, Mr. Bentley, who not only paid me handsomely for it, but secured my services as a regular
contributor to his magazine, ' Bentley's Miscellany.'
Later on he published my ' Cape and the Kaffirs,'
which had a great success, for I never saw a hostile
criticism of it, and many of them were only too
flattering.   The book was translated into French,
German, and Dutch, and reprinted in America.

Of course it is now obsolete, and I should be sorry
to pin my faith to all the statements and opinions it
contains.   Mr. Bentley was a dear old gentleman,
and had a fund of anecdote about literary men past
and present.   I recollect his telling me how Godwin,
the novelist, explained to him his method of framing
a novel.   It was first to devise a final catastrophe,

and thence to work back from cause to cause till he came to the starting-point.

" Very different," said Mr. Bentley, " from Dickens, who never has a plot at all, and you can see that he often alters his characters as he goes on from month to month."

But who reads ' Caleb Williams ' now? and 'how many of even educated men have even heard of it? Yet it was considered unmatched in Godwin's days. He was the father of Mrs. Shelley, the author of ' Frankenstein ' and the wife of the great poet.

Later on I wrote a novel called ' Lorimer Little-good,' which was illustrated by my dear old friend George Cruikshank, the great artist. As the work came out in monthly parts, I had each month to pay a visit to Cruikshank to decide on what should be the next illustration. I was a little fond of teasing the old gentleman, telling him that he had never been so great a caricaturist since he became a teetotaler. He stoutly denied this, and referred to his cartoon of ' The Bottle ' in refutation of it. I told him ' The Bottle ' was very clever, but not funny—on the contrary, somewhat ghastly and repulsive, to my taste. He often wished me to stay and dine with him ; but, as I had a horror of being obliged to eat plum-pudding washed down by cold water, I always excused myself.

Cruikshank had plenty of anecdotes concerning literary and artistic men, especially Dickens, of whom he was a profound admirer. It is known that Dickens never invented a proper name, but picked each one up from shop-fronts, the London Directory, and other sources.

One day Cruikshank and Dickens were walking together, and passed the cab-stand which is next to St. Martin's Church, Trafalgar Square. Two cabbies were chaffing one another, and one said to the other, " Oh, don't you come Oliver Twist over me!" Dickens exclaimed, "Did you hear that name? What a name!"—and he pulled out his pocket-book and wrote it down. I need not say that it became the title name of one of his greatest works, which was illustrated by Cruikshank himself. If I recollect, this was the only complete work of Dickens which Cruikshank did illustrate, but he did his work admirably upon it.

CHAPTER II.

Joined Cape Bar—Bench and Bar as they then were—First
Retainers—Circuits—Anecdote of Sir A. Cockburn.

I HAVE always agreed with Sir Walter Scott that
literature is a good walking-stick but a bad crutch;
that it is very well as an assistance, but except in the
case of great genius it does not do to rely on it for
one's exclusive support. So hearing at this time from
a brother of mine, then in the Colony, that there was
plenty of room for an advocate in the Supreme Court,
I determined to start for the Cape and try my fortune
there. There were no·steamers on the line in those
days, so I had to travel by a sailing-ship, which made
the passage in sixty days. However, I employed my
time in diligently studying Grotius, Van der Linden,
and other Roman-Dutch law authorities. I arrived in
the Colony in July, 1856, and was immediately afterwards sworn in and admitted as an advocate of the
Court.

I may here state what were the impressions I
formed of the appearance of the three judges who
then occupied the Bench. I am not speaking of
their intellectual qualifications, which were great,
but of their looks only.

The Acting Chief Justice, Mr. Bell, reminded me
of a respectable London butler out of place; Mr.
Justice Cloete, of a retired general with a dash of the
martinet temper in him; and Mr. Justice Watermeyer, of a prosperous English farmer or grazier.

The Registrar of the Court was Mr. Thomas Henry Bowles, an English barrister, a man of excellent family and a polished gentleman, though somewhat eccentric. It is said that a wicked lawyer's clerk once induced him when he was very busy at other Court work to sign his own death-warrant, commanding the sheriff to hang Thomas Henry Bowles by the neck till he was dead. The old gentleman used to reside in a small house in Grave Street, with no other companion or attendant than a venerable housekeeper. It is said that he never but once invited a friend to share his dinner.

The Master of the Court was Mr. Stewart, a man of ancient Scottish lineage, polished and courteous like the Registrar, but very reticent, except to a friend to whom he might take a fancy. I was fortunate enough to become one such, and he used to tell me the most amusing Scotch anecdotes. I never knew him laugh out loud, but he used to be convulsed with inward laughter, when his face would become crimson, making him look, as a friend of mine described it, like a dissipated old Punch.

The Interpreter was Mr. J. C. B. Serrurier, and an excellent one he was. He was very sensitive about the pronunciation of his name, strongly objecting to the " Sirringee " which many Dutchmen gave it. " If my name was the equivalent of ' Locksmith,' I don't think I should be particular about its pronunciation : I think I could be content with even ' Chubb.' "

. I must not forget the Usher of the Court, who used unconsciously to make the most hideous grimaces while listening to the arguments of counsel, or the judgments delivered from the Bench ; so that it was difficult for one who looked in his direction to keep from bursting into laughter.

The Bar consisted of Mr. William Porter, the Attorney-General, the most admirable orator I ever listened to in the Colony or in England. His face was handsome, his physique commanding, and his voice the most beautifully modulated I ever heard; but then I confess I never heard Spurgeon. Next came Mr. C. J. Brand, afterwards Sir Christoffel, and the first Speaker of the House of Assembly. He was a profoundly read Roman-Dutch lawyer, but never thoroughly mastered the English language or its accent, while he pronounced his Latin in true Dutch style, mercilessly throwing in all the gutterals. A listener declared that he heard him make seventeen false quantities in his quotations in an hour. Very likely. The Continentals do not care so much about quantities as the English, amongst whom, as Max O'Rell says, it is equivalent to the commission of a crime to make a false one.

Next came Mr. P. J. Denyssen, a good, amiable man who was rather proud of his English, which was really correct enough except for the overrolling of the letter ' r.' His Latin he pronounced in the style of the English public schools, having been principally taught it by a clergyman of the Church of England ; he was one of the best classics the Cape has ever known, and used to boast jokingly that he had had the satisfaction of caning two of the Judges on the Bench—Mr. Justice Denyssen and Mr. Justice Watermeyer, who had both been his pupils.

Next came Mr. J. H. Brand, afterwards Sir John Brand, the President of the Orange Free State. He

was deeply read in Roman-Dutch law, but profoundly
ignorant of literature in general; so that I doubt
whether he could have distinguished between a
quotation from Shakespeare and one from Dickens.
He was somewhat of a peppery temper (I used to call
him "firebrand"), but a really good, kind-hearted man,
and irreproachable in every domestic relation of life.

After him came Mr. R. B. Turner, commonly
called "Dick" by his friends—a very jolly fellow, an
Oxford M.A., and a barrister of Lincoln's Inn, but
perhaps with the most infinitesimal knowledge of
law ever possessed by a man professing to practise
at the profession.

I omitted the names of two gentlemen, who were,
however, seniors to all those I have referred to. The
one was Mr. William Hiddingh, still alive in his
eighty-ninth year, but who even in the days to which
I am referring possessed a fortune which made him
independent of practice. The other was a Mr. J. H.
Dreyer, who was really too nervous to practise. I
have seen, when he only had to mention a matter of
costs to the Bench, the paper trembling in his hand
to such an extent as to suggest a humanised sensitive
plant. Alas, all those I have mentioned, with this
one exception, have gone to that "country from
whose bourne no traveller returns"!

I received a few briefs in Cape Town, some of
them, I suppose, only complimentary; and then I
accepted an invitation—and retainers—of Mr. G.
Chabaud, a well-known solicitor of Port Elizabeth
and a distant relation of my own, to go to the
Circuit Courts of Port Elizabeth and Grahamstown.
So I took passage by sea to Algoa Bay. I was

successful beyond my expectations at both towns. I don't recollect that I lost a single case, while I know that I gained two or three of great importance. I looked upon my success at the Cape Bar as now assured; and I was right, for on my return to Cape Town the briefs poured in merrily. Perhaps I may mention here that Acting Chief Justice Mr. Bell was the presiding judge at the two Circuit Courts. He was the most wonderful combination of learning and ignorance I ever knew. I have heard him give judgments of great learning and research, and I have known him show ignorance which would shame a lawyer's clerk of three or four months' standing: thus in Grahamstown I had to defend the indorser of a promissory note on the ground that he had received no proper notice of dishonour.

" Did ye get ye notice ? " said the judge, who was very Scotch in his accent when he got excited.

" Yes, my lord, but only seven days instead of one after being dishonoured."

" But ye got ye notice ; so I think I must give notice against ye."

" Will your Lordship allow this case to be referred to the Supreme Court ? "

The Judge, contemptuously—" Certainly, if ye wish it ! "

To the Supreme Court, accordingly, the case went.

I stated what my defence had been, and the other two judges looked with some astonishment at Mr. Bell. A little whispering took place between the three judges, when Mr. Bell said—

" Was this the form in which the case came before me in Grahamstown ? "

"Yes, my lord ; if not, the fault must be mine "—
by way of soothing him.

Needless to add, the judgment was at once given
in my client's favour.

On another occasion I rose to re-examine my own
witness. The judge stopped me, saying—

" If ye want to put any other questions ye must
do it through the Court."

" Surely, my lord, I have a right to re-examine
my own witness after he has been cross-examined by
the other side ? "

" Where's ye authority for that ? "

My answer was, "I never expected to be called
upon for an authority upon so simple a matter."

" Then ye accept my ruling ? "

" On the contrary, my lord, I protest against it."

The judge twisted about, evidently irritated, and
asked the Registrar to hand him up ' Roscoe on Evidence '-in criminal cases. Having dived his spectacles
into the book, he said—

" I see ye're right ; but ye can't expect me to carry
all the law in my head, and 'protest' is a strong word
to use to the Bench."

The case then went on. It must not be supposed
from this that there was enmity between Judge Bell
and myself; on the contrary, we were very good
friends, and I often received very strong compliments
from him.

For my next Circuit trip I had received a retainer
from a well-known firm of solicitors in Port Elizabeth,
begging me to come up there some days before the
sitting of the Court in order to master the details of
a fire insurance case in which the amount involved
was £20,000 ; so I determined to try the post-cart.

In those days these carts were totally without cover or shelter of any kind, being simply a large box on wheels, with seats back and front *à la* dog-cart. Each was drawn by two horses, and driven almost entirely by coloured men, who divided their time into lashing their horses into a furious pace and falling asleep and letting them go as they wished. I several times had to take the reins, fearing a capsize. The roads were abominable, stony, and broken, and often quite dangerous. There were no stoppages except to change horses, and no possibility of getting any sleep, for to have attempted it would have been to have risked being thrown off and run over.

My original intention was to stop at Swellendam, a distance of about 144 miles from Cape Town, sleep there, and wait for the next cart—they started three times a week—then on to George, about an equal distance, sleep there, and wait again for the next cart, and thence on to Port Elizabeth. But on arriving at Swellendam I felt so lively, notwithstanding a rather cold night's drive, that I determined to push on by the same cart to George; again, on arriving at George, I felt well enough to go on without rest to Port Elizabeth. When I reached that place the landlord of the hotel to which I went greeted me with—

"Where from, sir?"

"Cape Town," I replied.

"Oh, yes, sir! But where from last?"

"Cape Town," I answered again.

"Do you mean to say that you have come right through without resting?"

"Certainly!" I said. "Three days and three nights with no rest, and very little to eat or drink."

"Good gracious!" he cried. "The only gentleman I have ever known do that was laid up for three
weeks at this hotel from fatigue."

"Now, landlord, give me a good warm bath, and
then a good breakfast, and I may take a nap; but I
have no intention of being laid up." Nor was I.

The great case for which I was retained was a very
interesting one. The plaintiff, a merchant in Port
Elizabeth, had had all the contents of his store de-
stroyed by fire, and claimed altogether £20,000 from
the various offices from which he was insured. The
companies resolved to amalgamate for the purpose of
defence, which was really that the store had not
contained any goods of that value. There was also
an insinuation of arson; but as it was not pleaded
no evidence could be taken on that matter.

The presiding judge was the new Chief Justice, Sir
William Hodges, then recently arrived from England.
He was a pleasant, good-natured man, somewhat like
a pork-butcher in appearance, but with no prejudices
—except, as a friend wrote from England—except
against the letter 'h,' and certainly that prejudice was
very strong. During the progress of our case offers
were made to us from the other side which the judge
kept warning us to consider seriously. At last came
an offer of £10,000. The judge said—

"I really think you ought to consult on this
matter."

We asked for an adjournment, and after about an
hour's consideration we returned into Court to
announce that we accepted the offer. Judgment
was entered accordingly.

To our great annoyance, we heard afterwards that

the judge had said at an evening party, "I think they should have stood out for more. If it had been left to me I think I should have given them £15,000." This was the more annoying because he had really all but driven us into accepting the compromise. But the matter was now past mending.

A somewhat humorous incident occurred during the trial. Mr. J. H. Brand, for the defendants, had called as a witness a Mr. Crump, a Grahamstown merchant, and the following conversation took place :—

" You were in the plaintiff's store, I believe, about two months before the fire occurred ? "

" Yes."

" What did you go there for ? "

" To see the plaintiff, who is an old friend of mine."

" You found him there ? "

" Yes."

" What did you do ? "

" Smoked a cigar with him."

" Did you notice the contents of the store ? "

" No."

" But you must have seen them."

" I suppose so; but seeing and noticing are two different things."

" Could you form any estimate of the value of the contents of the store ? "

" Not the remotest in the world ! "

" Then you know nothing at all about the case ? "

" Exactly so—nothing."

Mr. Brand flopped down in his seat somewhat irritated. The judge gave the usual nod to the witness to signify that he might go; but the latter

leant forward in the witness-box, and in the blandest
tones asked—

"My lord, am I at liberty to return to Grahamstown, as I have been detained here for some days at
great inconvenience?"

The Chief Justice said—

"Mr. Brand, do you think you will want this
witness any more?"

"No, my lord," growled the learned counsel.

The witness then, with a polite bow to both Bench
and Bar, left the Court. His coolness was delicious.

Sir William Hodges had not much legal learning,
as I have already said, and on his arrival in the
Colony his ignorance of Roman-Dutch law was complete. In endeavouring to make himself acquainted
with it, his defective scholarship offered an impediment, as he could not read the Latin authorities with
much facility. But he was a very pleasant companion,
and had been much liked by his brother barristers on
the Western Circuit in England. He had many good
anecdotes to tell, and amongst others was one of Sir
Alexander Cockburn, who was the leader of the Circuit,
and was very fond of Mr. Hodges. As I believe it has
never appeared in print, I shall give it here.

"Hodges," asked Cockburn, "have you ever heard
how I first got into good practice?" Hodges
replied—

"I have heard many stories about it, but I don't
know which is the true one."

"Well, then, I will tell you the correct one.

"Shortly after my call to the Bar, my uncle, the
Baronet, had a heavy Chancery suit connected with
his landed property. He expressed his wish to his

solicitor that I should hold the junior brief in the case. 'But,' said the solicitor, 'I believe your nephew had joined the Common Law Bar?'

"'Yes,' replied my uncle; 'but surely that does not prevent him from accepting a brief in a special case in the Court of Chancery?' 'No, it does not,' replied the solicitor; and so I got the brief. Although I was only to be junior in the case, I got up facts and arguments as if it all rested on me. The day before the suit was to be heard in the Lord Chancellor's Court I got a letter from my leader, saying that it was impossible for him to attend the next day, and urging me to go on by myself. I confess I was a little bit nervous about this; however, in the morning I took my seat in the Court. The suit being called on, I rose and told the Lord Chancellor that it was impossible for my leader to be present. The Chancellor—Lord Brougham—said, 'Go on with the case yourself, Mr. Cockburn; I'm sure you will do it every justice.' The solicitor urged me to do the same, and so I complied.

"I began carefully my statement of facts, and then proceeded to my arguments. The Chancellor at first listened to me with the greatest attention; but after a time I saw him take up sheet after sheet of litter-paper, evidently conducting a large private correspondence of his own, but I went on all the same. At the conclusion of my address the Lord Chancellor paid me some compliments, then shortly summed up the case, and gave judgment dead against me. This, you will say, was not very promising.

"But I may tell you that I had once or twice while addressing the Court noticed a most respectable old

C

gentleman with powdered hair and wearing tight
pantaloons and Hessian boots.   He was sitting on the
bench reserved for the solicitors, and was apparently
wrapped in attention to all my arguments, every
now and then glancing up at the Chancellor.

‹ " A month or two later I went on my first Circuit,
but hardly got a brief to speak of till I reached
St. Ives, in Cornwall.   Here some half-dozen briefs
were sent to me all endorsed with the name of the
same solicitor but one, which I did not recognise.
Then I got a request from the solicitor to fix a time for
a consultation.   He duly arrived, and, after puzzling
my mind for a minute or so, I recognised in him the
old gentleman I had seen in the Lord Chancellor's
Court.   I was very successful with his cases, winning,
I think, nearly every one of them ; and at the conclusion of the Circuit he thanked me warmly for my
attention to them.

"Next Circuit the same thing occurred—hardly any
briefs until I again got into Cornwall, where they
poured in as before from the same old gentleman.   I
afterwards heard that a friend of his had asked him
why he took such a fancy to me.

" ' My dear sir,' he replied, ' you don't know what
talent that young Cockburn has ! I happened to be
present when he argued, I think, his first case in the
Lord Chancellor's Court. I was greatly pleased ; and
so impressed was the Lord Chancellor that he hardly
ceased from taking notes of the counsel's arguments.'

"He had evidently mistaken the private letters
which the Chancellor was writing for notes of my
speech. However, his mistake stood me in good
stead, for it not only brought me the briefs in

question, but next Circuit a flood of them from all parts on our route. I had established my reputation."

Sir Alexander was a man of great frankness. On one occasion he had a brief in a great trespass case connected with some property in Cambridgeshire. A brother of mine, who was his junior, had carefully worked up the diagrams and plans of the estate, and in consultation proceeded to explain them to Cockburn.

" Don't trouble yourself, Mr. Cole," he said; " I know every inch of the property: I poached over it many a time when I was at the University."

His splendid oratory told rather against him with the attorneys, who are apt to fancy that a brilliant speaker must be but a poor lawyer. So when he was appointed Chief Justice of England many were the prophecies that he would be a dead failure on the Bench; but he disappointed them all and became, I think, the greatest English Chief Justice of the present century; while his judgment in the famous arbitration case in Geneva between England and the United States, and in which he differed from his colleagues, stamped him as a man of unsurpassed ability. I think almost every Englishman acknowledges that he was right, and even the Yankees don't care to discuss the question.

CHAPTER III.

Travelling—A Capsize—Small-pox Scare—Queer Night Quarters
—Practical Jokers.

THE usual method of travelling Circuit when I joined the Bar, and for some years afterwards, was for each man to have his own cart and horses, the cart carrying himself and driver, his luggage, and a certain supply of provisions for the road. The start was made at sunrise. After two or two-and-a-half hours' journeying we outspanned for breakfast, knee-haltering the horses, and letting them graze and get water. Meantime our servants collected fuel, of which there was generally plenty about, made a fire, and set on the kettle to boil, and also on a gridiron on the ashes cooked some chops, or a dish of eggs and some toast. When we had breakfasted we smoked our cigars. This all took an hour or more, when we inspanned and started again for about the same time as in the first instance, when we again outspanned for lunch. This generally consisted of cold provisions, potted meats, &c., and a bottle of Bass. Then we started again until we arrived at the inn or other place where we were to have dinner and spend the night. We were generally expected at this place, and got very decent fare. Next day we went through the same process, till we reached the Circuit town for which we were bound. These journeys were on the whole by no means unpleasant, although some of us growled at their monotony and the slow pace, which seldom exceeded more than six miles an hour. It was, however, rather an expensive way of travelling, costing each man about two guineas a day, besides his servants' wages, wear and tear of cart and harness, and the occasional sickness of his horses. When this occurred the only thing was to sell the pair—generally for about half the price they had cost you—and buy a new pair.

In this way I had once to leave no less than three pair of horses behind me, and the result was a big hole in my fees. Sometimes two men would join in the same cart. I did this once myself, with my friend Dick Turner, who, however, was only going part of the Circuit, while I was bound for the whole. On our journey we had a little adventure. Leaving Grahamstown for Fort Beaufort, Turner, who was driving, struck on a new road which was being made; but the workman suddenly ran forward, crying, "You can't pass—the road is not finished!"

Turner hurriedly pulled his horses to turn back, but unfortunately dropped one rein, which caused the horses to twist back suddenly, upsetting the cart bottom upwards, and running some yards with it in that position. Turner and I and the groom were, of course, thrown out sprawling on the ground.

A good-natured English farmer came running towards us, asking whether we were hurt. We assured him that with the exception of a few scratches we were undamaged. Upon this he put his hands on his knees, and burst into shouts of laughter, crying—

" And a couple of lawyers too ! "—for he knew us.

He seemed to think it the greatest piece of fun in the world to see a couple of lawyers capsized. We then went on our way, the horses, which were naturally a lively pair, being greatly excited by the accident.

After reaching a certain town Turner left me to return to Cape Town by post-cart, and I became coachman for the rest of the journey. It was the only journey in which I fell in with a severe snow-storm, which lasted two whole days, and, as I had foolishly brought no overcoat with me except the old style of glazed mackintosh, it may be imagined I was not particularly warm. The storm went on till I reached the Oude Berg, on the other side of which lies Graaf Reinet, when it began to turn to sleet, and then to rain, until, descending to the town itself, I got into perfectly fine weather.

It must be remembered that in those days there was but one Circuit for the whole Colony, starting from Cape Town and reaching all the way to Aliwal North, then the Ultima Thule of the Colony, and thence turning back through Colesberg, Burghersdorp, &c., and thence by the Great Karoo home.

In many parts of the country we got very poor accommodation, and had to rough it a good deal. I have often slept for the night in the open air lying on the sand in the Karoo. But I must confess I slept soundly. The farmers, as a rule, were very hospitable. On one occasion, however, we were a little thrown out in our calculations. I had a cart and four horses, as my wife was travelling with me. We were leaving by our usual road from Burghersdorp

on the way to Colesberg. Coming to a certain point
of the road, we were going to take the usual turn to
a farmer's house, which we had been accustomed to
visit, but found it blocked with stones across it.
Thinking that they must have made a new road up
to the house further on, we jogged resignedly along ;
but no such new road was to be found ; we therefore
struck away by another route, making sure of finding
another farmhouse. It became quite dark before we
found any such place ; but after a time we heard the
sound of people talking, evidently Kaffirs. Fortunately, one of our party was an attorney who
spoke Kaffir as well as English. He called to the
speakers in their native language and asked them
where we were. They told us it was a Mr. ——'s
place, but that he and all his family were away
from home, and had removed all the furniture of the
house with them. However, they allowed us to
enter the house, from which even the doors of the
rooms had been removed ; but my wife discovered
one door lying down, and it was unanimously resolved
to make it our table. One of our servants had a
candle, and I proposed that we should tap a bottle of
Bass and use the bottle as a candlestick. Then we
got in the cushions from our carts, overcoats,
wrappers, etc., and we managed to get wood enough
from the Kaffirs, with which we made a fire on the
hearth of what appeared to be the principal sitting-
room. All of us then contributed our stock of provisions, which was but a scanty one after all, and
then proceeded to make our supper off them. So
far from being at all put out, my wife enjoyed the
fun of the adventure greatly. The sitting-room was

assigned to us as our bedroom, and the others occupied different smaller rooms.

Somehow or another we managed to sleep through the night pretty well, until, at the very peep of day, we again started on our journey. It was a lovely morning, and we enjoyed the very pretty sight of seeing the springboks start from the ground where they had been sleeping, and after a few bounds in the air turning round to look at us with curiosity, for it was a very unfrequented road, and they were unaccustomed to the sight of such a cavalcade as our party formed.

I may here mention that there had been an outbreak of small-pox in the Colony, and that there were two cases of it in the hospital about a mile outside Burghersdorp, from which place we last hailed ; thus we were looked on by the farmers as dangerous infected people. This had led to the closing of the road which we had intended to take, and I believe also to the bolting of the farmer from the place we had just quitted. The Boers were terribly afraid of the disease, and, considering the ravages it had once created in Cape Town, when nearly a third of the Malay population was swept away by it, one can hardly be surprised at their nervousness.

We pushed on very hungry, making for a farm which we were accustomed to visit in order to get breakfast there. On arriving we saw only one man —a son of the house—who looked very frightened, especially when Mr. Denyssen, one of our party, who knew him, shook him by the hand. I think he looked upon himself then as doomed to the *pokkies*, as the Boers call it. The house, though containing plenty of inhabitants, was locked up to prevent our entering it, with the exception of one room, which had apparently been forgotten, and into this one we made our entrance.

Mr. Denyssen explained to the farmer that we wanted breakfast, as we had had but a poor supper the night before, and were very hungry. But the man seemed powerless to help us. My wife, who spoke Cape Dutch very well, took up the matter, and told the man in tones loud enough to be heard by the rest of the people in the house that we should not go away till we had had breakfast. This somewhat frightened them, and the old lady of the house was heard exclaiming, "This is shameful—fancy taking one's house like that!" Then, apparently to a servant, "Watch until they are all out of the room, and then lock the door." But we were too smart for that, and took care that whoever might leave the room there should be always one left in it. A servant afterwards made her appearance, keeping, however, a long way off. My wife called to her, "Get us some breakfast at once! We shall not leave the house till we have it."

A conference apparently ensued between the mistress and maid; and the latter after a time cried out, still keeping a long way off, "There's breakfast ready in the next room," the door of which she had left open. We got a very fair meal, and were hungry enough to dispose of it. Then Mr. Denyssen settled with his friend for the forage and the breakfast, and we jogged along on our way to Colesberg, only about two hours distant.

We afterwards heard that the poor man who had

shaken hands was locked out of the house and refused admission. But the judge, Mr. Justice Cloete, arrived in the place the same evening, and, finding how matters stood, addressed the man, saying, " I shall order my people to help my horses to the forage they require ; you may starve me if you like, and I can sleep in my waggon." Then he harangued the man about the cruelty, inhumanity, and want of Christian feeling shown by him and the rest of the people in the place, and told them that God would certainly punish them for it.

The old gentleman's eloquence produced its effect, for one by one the inmates came out of the house and begged him to forgive them, which after a show of resistance he did. He got a capital dinner, and slept comfortably that night.

Before leaving the subject of small-pox, I may relate how two young scamps took advantage of the scare for their own amusement. They got a cart and horses and drove about the country, generally seeking out remote farm-houses. The farmer, seeing their approach, would come out of the house holding up his hands and shouting, " You can't come here— you can't come here ! " In return they cried out, " But we are doctors come to vaccinate you, and prevent you from getting the *pokkies*."

Then the farmer's tone changed.

" Come in then at once ! "—which they did ; and in a short time one arm of every inmate of the house was bared for the operation. Then the two young fellows took out a bottle of curdled sour milk, and, dipping their penknives into it, proceeded to " vaccinate " the people. Whether they took money for this I cannot say, but they certainly got the best eating and drinking which the farmers could provide for them.

One of these young gentlemen, whom I will call Mr. S., some time afterwards played another game. He was in the town or village of George, whether on business or otherwise I do not know. A rumour got abroad that he was a celebrated English barrister who was having a look at the country before settling to practise in it. A Dutch farmer whom I remember very well, hearing this report, went to the hotel where Mr. S. was staying, and asked to see him. He was admitted, and then proceeded to tell in Cape Dutch his complaint about an assault to which he had been subjected, and for which he wished to bring an action in the George Circuit Court. It never seems to have struck him as strange that a newly arrived English barrister should have a perfect command of the Cape Dutch, as Mr. S. certainly had. His story was shortly that, being in the bar of a hotel in the place, he got into a quarrel with two other men, who then attacked him, knocked him about, and tore off one tail of his coat, for he wore a long-tailed coat in honour of some festive meeting. Mr. S. kept using pen and ink while the story went on, and at the end of it produced a capital sketch—for he was a skilful draughtsman—in which he had made a very good likeness of his client, and a fancy sketch of two other men in the act of tearing off the coat-tail.

Now he said—" I suppose if one of your Cape advocates had your case he would make a long speech to the judge describing how things happened ; but that's not the way we do it in England now. I hand up this sketch to the judge, and say, ' There, my lord, you can see how it all happened '—it saves a great deal of time."

" But that's capital ! "

" Well, now remember the Circuit Court sits here in about a fortnight—so don't be too late."

" No, mynheer," said the farmer ; " but how much have I to pay, mynheer ? "

" Oh, " said S., " I won't take any money from you at present, but you may stand half-a-dozen champagne if you like."

" Certainly," said the farmer, and the wine was soon forthcoming.   They drank a bottle of it together, and then the farmer took his departure, Mr. S. consigning the other five bottles to his travelling-cart.

When the Circuit came on, needless to say, no Mr. S. was to be found, no one knew whence he came, nor where he had gone ; so the poor farmer had still to bewail the loss of his coat-tail and of the money he had spent on the champagne.

CHAPTER IV.

Mr. Justice Cloete—Telling a Horse's Age—General Sir A. J. Cloete—His Greeting by the old Duke of Cambridge.

MR. JUSTICE CLOETE was a man of remarkable ability; he was not only a lawyer of great learning, but a man of good literary taste, and of course his command of the Dutch and English languages was perfect. He was fond of telling anecdotes, and some of them were very amusing. When at the University of Leyden, where he took his degree, he had as fellow-students two twin brothers, so perfectly like one another in face, figure, voice, and height that even their own parents could not distinguish one from the other. The young fellows took advantage of this resemblance, and always dressed precisely alike. The consequence was that if a complaint to the University authorities was made against either of them the accuser was confronted with two, and asked to point out which one it was, and this he could not do, and so both escaped, as it would have been unjust to punish the innocent and guilty alike.

On one occasion one of the brothers, who had been unshaved three or four days, entered a barber's shop and asked to be operated on. The barber at once handed him a seat.

"But," said the young gentleman, "are you sure you can shave quite clean, so that I shall not have my beard sticking out again in two or three hours?"

"Oh, you may be quite sure of that!" said the barber, laughing, and the shaving took place.

Two or three hours later the other brother came into the shop with a four days' beard on him.

"Look here, now—is this what you call clean shaving?"

"Good heavens!" cried the barber, throwing up his hands. "Is it possible for a man's beard to grow so fast as that?"

Of course, he hadn't the least doubt that it was the man he had shaved three or four hours before.

When first joining the Cape Bar Mr. Cloete received a brief to defend a man charged with murder; it looked a very ugly case, and he had little hope of success; but, to his surprise, the man was acquitted. He went home delighted to tell his parents of what had happened. An old English Colonel, who was staying in the house, said—

"Well, Cloete, I have lived two or three years in this country, and my belief is that it requires a devilish good deal of interest to get hanged in it."

Mr. Cloete was for some time the Recorder of Natal, which was then a Crown Colony dependent on the Cape, and he was much liked and respected there. On one occasion he had to preside at the trial of a man charged with very serious assault. Among the witnesses called for the Crown were two— a man named Murphy and a woman named Mrs. McGrath. The evidence of the former was very clear; but the woman confessed that she had been asleep for a considerable time during which the disturbance had been committed. Summing up the case to the jury, the judge said—

"Murphy's evidence is clear enough; but I don't think you can rely much on that of Mrs. McGrath, because according to her own account she was for some time in the arms of Morpheus"—the god of sleep.

"Me lad, me lad," shouted the woman, standing up in Court, "plaze doon't take away my character like that! I never was in Murphy's arms in my life!"

The judge was somewhat of an irritable temper; but a few soft words always smoothed him down, and, if he showed any irritation with the counsel whom he thought wandered from the point, he was always ready to apologise when he found out his mistake. He once while at the Bar challenged the late Mr. Justice Menzies—dead some years before I came into the Colony—for real or fancied insult; but the judge refused the challenge, and Mr. Cloete had to let his anger quietly cool down.

He would have made a capital soldier, being a man of great courage, who never shirked any danger which presented itself while travelling on Circuit. His next brother, General Sir Josias Cloete, K.C.B., &c., had joined it in early life. He never married till he was more than sixty-five years of age, and had two children by his wife, a son and a daughter. He lived to see the former a captain in the Artillery, and his daughter married to a man of good position in England. He died at the age of ninety-five, "the father of the British Army."

On first joining the Service he was gazetted to a crack Hussar regiment, the Colonel-in-Chief of which was the late Duke of Cambridge, father of the present one. His Royal Highness once paid his regiment a visit, and desired that each of his officers should be presented to him. When it came to the name of Cornet A. J. Cloete he looked puzzled, and asked—

" What are your Christian names, sir ? "

" Abraham Josias," was the reply.

The Duke started, and said—

" Then, damme, sir, you must be a Jew ! "

" No, your Royal Highness," was the reply, " I am a Christian, and a Dutchman of the Cape of Good Hope."

" Oh, I see, I see, I see ! "—repeating his words in the fashion of his father, George III.

By the way, the Duke had another peculiarity—a habit of thinking aloud. Thus I once heard him at the church service at the Foundling Hospital when the clergyman spoke the words, " Let us pray," cry out—" Quite right ! Let us pray—let us pray " —dropping reverently on his knees while he uttered the words, which must have been heard by at least half the congregation present.

Amongst his other accomplishments, Mr. Justice Clocte was a first-rate judge of a horse, and this fact was recognised by nearly all the farmers of the western districts of the Colony. On one occasion he had to cross the Gouritz River, through which the main road to Riversdale passes. The river was bridgeless, and at that time full. There was a punt large enough to convey a few passengers and a vehicle, but not the horses—these had to be driven to swim the river. On reaching the farther side of the river, the judge was met by a large number of farmers, mostly mounted, who had assembled to greet him. One of them, who, as the judge said, was " *Beetje lekker* "—or, as we should say, a little bit " on "— called to him—

" Now, Mynheer Clocte, I know you are a capital

judge of a horse. Tell me how old this one is that I am riding."

The judge saw at a glance that the horse was too old to make it of any use to look at his mouth; so he walked up to his tail and began separating the hairs of it, and apparently making mental notes. Thinking, as he afterwards told me, like Rory O'More, that there is luck in odd numbers, he said—

"Well, I should say that horse is nineteen years of age."

The rider cried—

"*Alamachte!* He is exactly nineteen; I bred him myself."

Thereupon all the rest crowded round the judge, asking him "to let them know how he could tell a horse's age from his tail."

The judge shook his head and said—

"No, no—that is my secret!"

So they had to go away unenlightened; but I believe there are farmers in that neighbourhood who to this day declare that Judge Cloete could tell a horse's age from his tail.

As I happen to have married the niece of the judge and general—*par nobile fratrum*—of whom I have been speaking, it may be thought that I write with some prejudice in their favour. It may be so, but I am unconscious of it.

D

CHAPTER V.

Judge Watermeyer—Judge Menzies—A Snowy Outspan—A Ticklish Journey through Hex River Pass.

THE ablest and most learned judge who has occupied the Cape Bench in my time was, I think, Mr. Justice Watermeyer. He was not only a deeply read lawyer but an excellent classic, and had much literary taste. When I was editor, conjointly with the late Professor Roderic Noble, of the 'Cape Monthly Magazine,' he used to send as translations in English verse the epigrams of Martial, admirably done. I remember that when he sent in the last one he wrote: "I think I have now sent you a translation of every *decent* epigram that Martial ever wrote; the rest, of course, I cannot touch."

He was a man of wonderful self-control; his attacks of the gout were fearful. I have seen him carried into the Court in Grahamstown unable to put his foot to the ground, and evidently in torment, yet he sat perfectly quiet, and, though the writhing of his features often showed the agony he was suffering, he never uttered an angry or impatient word, and did a whole day's work without a complaint. Shakespeare says—

> "For never yet was there philosopher
> That could patiently endure the toothache."

I should have thought it was more difficult still to

patiently endure the gout, yet the judge did it. His judgments were very lucid and logical, and expressed in the most apt language, which was the more remarkable because he suffered from a slight impediment of speech, which he did his best to resist and overcome, and to a great extent succeeded, but it made his sentences when listened to sound rather " choppy," if I may so express it; but when read in print it was seen how perfect was their construction.

I have said that he was a good classic, and his brother, Mr. Fred Watermeyer, afterwards a member and an ornament of the Cape Bar, was equally so. The brothers used to correspond with one another in Greek for the sake of practice. I have never known men except these two, who are not Greeks by birth, write letters of that language.

He had a great admiration for a former judge, Mr. Justice Menzies, whom he considered the greatest lawyer the Cape ever saw; but he tells some funny stories about him.

At a Circuit Court held by him the prisoner was asked the usual question, whether he objected to be tried by any of the jurymen who were then sworn in. He answered—

" No, I don't mind being tried by them, but I don't want to be tried by that little fellow up there " —pointing to Judge Menzies on the bench. There was a burst of laughter, in which the judge heartily joined.

Entering the Circuit Court on another occasion, he saw a young advocate seated with a row of books before him for the purpose of quotation.

" Ye don't mean to say, sir "—looking angrily at

D 2

the barrister—" that ye're going to read all those books to *me* ? "

Which was hardly encouraging to a young advocate. The truth is, he had a great contempt for authorities which did not coincide with his own opinion. A counsel once quoted to him a case decided in the Queen's Bench in England.

" Well, sir, and if the Court of Queen's Bench chooses to lay down bad law, am I bound to follow it ? "

He certainly was a very irritable man.

Occasionally, too, he made mistakes like others. After the decision of an important suit known as the " Scorey Case," he went to the Chambers of Mr. William Porter, whom he greatly admired and respected.

" Porter," he said, " I've been thinking over that ' Scorey Case.' Tell me, were such and such facts " —naming them—" proved at the trial ? "

" They were certainly not," said Mr. Porter.

" Then what the devil made us give the judgment we did ? "

I got this anecdote from Mr. Porter himself. The coolness and apparent insensibility of Mr. Menzies to the feelings of other people were often manifest. It is said that he once passed sentence of death on a murderer ending with the usual words, " And may the Lord have mercy on your soul! " Without hesitating for a moment he went on—" Go on with the next case! "

He once took the extraordinary step of leaving his Circuit Court at Colesberg, riding across to the Orange River, crossing the boundary into what is now the Orange Free State, and annexing that country in the name of Her Majesty and declaring it British territory, which, of course, he had no more right to do than the meanest of Cape colonists.

Judge Watermeyer was a great admirer also of Mr. Porter, and the admiration was mutual. Mr. Porter once wrote of him : " Of so vast ability that he could have succeeded without industry, and of so great an industry that he could almost have succeeded without ability."

He also gave him credit for unconsciousness of his own merits; but here I think he was mistaken: my impression always was that the judge and his brother were both thoroughly conscious of their talents, though they were never guilty of any particular display of vanity.

The judge had a good fund of humour and wit; but after he had made use of either he had a habit of appearing to shrink into himself, as if he had forfeited a little bit of his dignity, which was surely a mistake.

The Circuit party were once outspanned on the top of what might almost be called a mountain, and the snow was thick upon the ground, making us all very lively, and Mr. Gustavus Chabaud, who was one of us, threw off his hat, as he always did when he got excited, and trudged about in the snow, making me say, in some verses I wrote on the occasion—

> " And Mr. Chabaud
> Without his *chapeau*
> Running about and enjoying the snow."

Said Judge Watermeyer to me—

"Why, Cole, this is *nix*" (snow). A play upon the Dutch word *niets*, meaning "nothing."

I have already said that snow is very rare in the Colony; but coming home once from the Karroo I had to make my way up a mountain pass called Hottentot's Kloof, and the road and the country around were covered with snow a foot or two deep. I got out of the cart partly to make it lighter for the horses and partly to keep myself warm by exercise. I felt terribly inclined to make some snowballs and pitch them at my old coachman, who sat doubled up with cold; but it struck me that he might think I had gone mad, and so whip up his horses and gallop away from me, leaving me in the road entirely alone; so discretion prevailed over inclination.

Travelling in company with the same judge and sharing a cart with Mr. Denyssen, we arrived at the top of the Hex River heights—there was then, of course, no railway. At this spot a farmer arrived with a span-team of splendid horses in order to convey the judge to Worcester, where we were bound, the judge having formerly been a member of the House of Assembly for the division of Worcester, where he was extremely popular. Seeing that there were more horses than necessary for a judge, we asked the farmer whether he could not let us have a pair to put in as leaders to our own cart; he had no objection provided we had a driver whom we could trust, as among the odd horses there was no pair that had been driven as leaders, nor as wheelers, but only in the centre of the team, which commonly enough consists of eight or ten horses. The judge lent us his coachman, a Malay, and probably the best driver in the Colony, so the two borrowed horses were spanned in as our leaders. There was a wide stretch of level grassy ground there, round which Hermanus drove the cart by himself, begging us to be ready at the drift of the river we had to cross. When he came to us we jumped in and made for the drift; but the leaders were so wild that they swerved from the drift and plunged into the river, where it was of considerable depth, and where there were large boulders which threatened to capsize the cart or smash it. But somehow we got safely across, and then started up the road, which was scarped out of the mountain and had a low parapet wall on the off-side of it. The leaders were still quite mad, and after a time they jumped clean over the little parapet wall on to the top of a precipice. Denyssen sprang out to save his life, and I was about to follow his example, when the driver cried, "Sit still, Mr. Cole! I promise you, you shall not be hurt!" So I kept my seat, and by dint of skilful handling of the reins and of the whip Hermanus actually made the horses jump back again into the road, shaking and trembling all over, for they had evidently got frightened at their own rashness.

After picking up Mr. Denyssen we went forward again, the leaders still being fidgety and unruly; but our coachman managed them so well that long before we got to Worcester they were as quiet as lambs, and fit to be excellent leaders in future.

Although Mr. Justice Watermeyer—for his family was of German origin—had certainly not a drop of English blood in his veins, he was a thorough Englishman in habits and taste. Completely master of the languages of Holland and England, he detested Cape Dutch. I have still in my possession a letter of his on the subject of education addressed to a friend in Graaff Reinet, and by the latter handed to me. In it he writes: "One of the greatest drawbacks to progress of our colonial youth in learning is their habit of constantly speaking and thinking in that no-language, Cape Dutch. It is impossible for any one to think deeply or to express himself lucidly in this style. It ought to be repressed as soon as possible among the boys."

And yet what have we been doing for the last twenty years? Petting and cherishing the *taal* as if it were something precious and sacred, instead of a grammarless *patois*. The result has been a distinctly retrograde movement in legislation and education alike. I know there is a distinguished gentleman living who has expressed his liking for Cape Dutch, and has written amusing translations in it from Burns and other authors; but I don't believe he can seriously look upon it as a vehicle for the thoughts of intelligent and highly educated men.

CHAPTER VI.

Mr. Justice Bell and his Peculiarities.

AMONGST the peculiarities of Mr. Justice Bell was a habit of taking strong prejudices in favour of or against certain persons. The prejudices were generally, I think, unaccountable. Thus he would take a great fancy to people whom I should have considered very unattractive, and on the other hand a violent dislike to agreeable and intelligent people. As an instance of the latter, he always showed great animosity to the late Mr. Buyskes, a Clerk of the Peace of Graaff Reinet. It was the duty of Clerks of the Peace in those days to prosecute in criminal cases in the Circuit Courts, each division of the Colony having such an officer. The practice has long been abolished, and the conduct of these cases is now entrusted to barristers only. Mr. Buyskes, to my mind, used to do his work very fairly; but I suppose the judge was not of the same opinion. On one occasion, during the progress of a case, a witness for the Crown having given his evidence, Mr. Justice Bell turned to the prisoner and asked him—

"Now, what do you say to that?"

Of course it was illegal for the judge to ask him any questions at all. The prisoner muttered some reply.

"Ah, but ye see," said the judge, "the witness

says so and so. What have ye got to answer to that ? "

Just then he happened to catch sight of Mr. Buyskes, who was talking smilingly to some friends around him.

" Mr. Clerk of the Peace, I wish you would attend to what is going on in the Court ! "

" I am attending."

" No, sir, ye are not ! What was I doing ? "

" Cross-examining the prisoner, my lord."

The judge threw himself back in his chair as if he was shot—a trick he always had when taken by surprise—but he made no reply. I suppose it struck him suddenly that this was exactly what he had been doing—a thoroughly illegal proceeding.

At another Circuit Court at Graaff Reinet, he sent a message to Mr. Buyskes to attend him in his private room during the adjournment. When Buyskes arrived there the judge addressed him—

" I wish, Mr. Buyskes, you would dress with propriety when you come into Court."

Buyskes looked himself all over and was quite puzzled. He said—

" I know, my lord, that according to the regulations I am entitled to wear a barrister's gown when prosecuting, but I have always thought it a piece of presumption on the parts of Clerks of the Peace to assume that costume."

" That's not what I mean, sir," said the judge ; " but you ought to wear a white tie, and not a black one."

" I'm very sorry, my lord, but really I don't possess one ; but I will take care to provide one for the occasion of your lordship's next visit here "—and he walked away.

The same judge dealt with another Clerk of the Peace in much more humorous fashion. This was at Worcester, and the gentleman, whose name I forget, was the last of the Clerks of the Peace. Wishing, I suppose, to impress the Bench with his learning, he ventured to quote in the original Latin a passage from Voet; but he read it in such style that the judge at once guessed that he did not understand the meaning of the words he was citing.

" Give me the English of that," said the judge.

The gentleman hesitated, and looked confused.

" Give me the English of that," repeated the judge.

" I—I—I beg your lordship's pardon ! I—I thought you understood Latin."

" Oh, no, I don't ! Do you ? "

The man was utterly confounded.

" It's a pity," said the judge, " you make yourself so ridiculous."

And the poor man sat down utterly abashed.

Judge Bell was a very temperate man, and he told me that the only thing he liked was an occasional glass of sweet wine—my own special abomination. He was giving us a dinner at George, and a bottle of claret was placed on the table; it was abominably " corked," and each man as he tasted it at once put down his glass. The judge, who would not have known whether the wine was " corked " or not, looking round the table, said, " Well, as I see, gentlemen, you don't want any more wine "—which was exactly what we did want, but we wanted it sound—" we had better adjourn to the next room for coffee." I think if I had been the senior barrister instead of the junior one I should have explained the truth of the matter to his lordship.

He presided at a Circuit Court at Queenstown, where the mayor and town council invited the whole of us to a dinner. A heavy case of murder prolonged the sitting of the Court to something like half-past eight, when we were all able to make an appearance at table. The judge was terribly fatigued, and asked one of the waiters to bring him a glass of ale. The obsequious waiter filled a tumbler and handed it to him, and he had sent three parts of it down his throat before he discovered that it was sherry he was swallowing, and not ale. This made him very drowsy indeed, and I don't know how he managed to eat his dinner.

When his health was proposed by the mayor, he seemed to me to be sound asleep, but, to my surprise, he got up and returned thanks in a manner which showed that he had heard every word that had been said.

Riding with him once along the Rondebosch road, I made some remark about Cape sheep, which have enormously fat tails.

"There's a similar breed in Central India," he said; "it's a wise provision of nature."

"To make dripping, I suppose?"

"No, Cole," he said, "of course not, but to preserve their lives."

He was quite right, for it is true that these sheep can live without food or water for a very long time on their own fat, their tails greatly diminishing during this mode of existence.

The judge was really a kind-hearted man, but very eccentric, and was apt to be rude and overbearing in his manner and language. This led our Attorney-General, Mr. Porter, to say to him in full Court that his manner towards the Bar was felt to be very offensive. The great reputation and stately manner of the speaker took him aback.

"I never meant to be offensive," he said.

"No," replied Mr. Porter, "we do not accuse your lordship of *intending* to annoy us, but your language and manner are often found to be irritating and offending."

The judge apologised and the matter ended; but he certainly was more guarded in his language in the future.

The judge was decidedly "hard of hearing," and this once led to a curious mistake. A prisoner had been tried before him in Grahamstown, and the jury returned a verdict of "Guilty."

"The prisoner is discharged," said the judge, to the surprise of all the Court. But the dock was opened, and the prisoner made the best of his way out of Court and out of town. The registrar stood up and said—

"But, my lord, the jury said 'Guilty.'"

"No, no—'Not guilty,'" said the judge. "Gentlemen, what was your verdict?"

"Guilty, my lord," was the reply.

"Oh," he replied, "fetch the man back!"

And immediately three or four policemen might be seen flying down the High Street in hot pursuit. But I believe they never captured the runaway.

A prisoner once arraigned before him being

asked the usual question, "Guilty, or not guilty?" replied—

"That's just what you've got to find out."

This so irritated the judge that he told him he should give him an extra month's imprisonment for contempt of Court. But was it contempt of Court? Did not the man simply express in words what is the intention of nineteen out of twenty prisoners who plead "Not guilty"?

This reminds me of an anecdote concerning Judge Menzies, told me by the late Sir John Brand, who, I believe, was present on the occasion it refers to. A prisoner, who had pleaded "Not guilty," was, after a short trial, convicted by the jury. Passing a severe sentence on him, the judge said—

"Ye're not only guilty, but ye come here and tell lies, saying ye are not."

The next prisoner on the roll of trial, hearing these words, thought he would please the judge, and so, when called upon to plead, said boldly, "Guilty, my lord."

"Oh, guilty you are, is it?" said the judge. "And you come here to brag of it, do you?"

And he gave him as severe a sentence as the last one. It must have been difficult to conciliate such a judge as that.

CHAPTER VII.

Terrific Thunderstorm—Three Days at Roadside Inn—Queenstown Gaol.

THUNDERSTORMS and hailstorms, although comparatively rare in the Cape peninsula, are frequent,
severe, and dangerous in most other parts of the
Colony. It has been my lot to travel through a few
of them. I was leaving a town two hours later one
morning than the other barristers, having been detained for a consultation. I went along for about
two hours, and then outspanned to feed and rest my
horses, and take a little refreshment myself. Heavy
black clouds hung all round, and it was clear that I
was in for a storm, so I begged my driver to get
ready for a start at once. We had gone a very little
way when there was a brilliant flash of lightning and
a peal of thunder ahead of us. Directly afterwards
came another flash and peal on our right hand, and
in a short time we were in the centre of the most
furious thunderstorm I have ever known. The
lightning was blinding and the thunder deafening,
nor was there the slightest interval between flash
and peal. I expected every moment that we must
be struck, for my cart was almost the only object
above the level of the ground, which was a vast plain,
with not a tree or shrub upon it. I made my coachman put the horses to a hard gallop, knowing that a
swiftly-moving vehicle was less liable to be struck

than one standing still or moving slowly. Suddenly
the rain came down in torrents such as I have
never seen before. The road, which was only an
inch or two below the grass surrounding it, was at
once converted into a rivulet, and we ourselves were
speedily wet through to the skin, in spite of all the
overcoats and wrappers we could lay hands on. By
the flashes of lightning we could see before us the
roadside inn to which we were making at least half
or three-quarters of an hour's ride before we could
get there; but as we approached nearer to it I
noticed that there was a slight interval between the
flash and the peal, which showed me that the storm
was passing a little away from us. When at last we
reached the house and dashed round the corner to
the front of it, startling some people assembled under
the veranda watching the storm, they seemed to
think we had fallen from the clouds. The inn was
on the banks of the Klaas-Smits River, and below it
was a ford or drift across the stream. I learned that
my friends had crossed this stream about two hours
before, the water being scarcely deep enough to cover
their horses' fetlocks—it was now a raging torrent, full
twelve to fifteen feet deep, with a roar rivalling that
of the thunder, and sweeping down with it trunks of
trees, carcasses of oxen and sheep—in fact, everything
it came in contact with. It was a grand sight, but
a very unpleasant one to a traveller.

In the small inn here I was destined to pass nearly
three whole days; but the people were very attentive,
and did all they could to make me comfortable, and
I had two consolations: first, I found there 'Tom
Cringle's Log,' a book which I had never yet read. It

was a godsend, for I had used up all my travelling stock of literature; and, secondly, I was joined by the field cornet, who had come there to meet the judge. He was an Englishman, a gentleman, and well educated—very unlike the generality of these officials. Of course we chummed together, talked together, and made ourselves as happy as we could under difficulties.

On the third day the rain ceased, and the river seemed to have in a very slight degree subsided; but still it was totally impassable. Mr. Ella, the field cornet, then told me that he knew a drift some miles lower down the river, which he thought might perhaps be passable; so we spanned in our carts and started for it. When we reached the spot it looked a little ugly, but not so bad as the drift we had left behind us. I suddenly noticed some Kaffirs on the other side coming towards the river. They waded through the drift, and came up the bank on our side. I led one of them up to my cart, raising it as it would be when the horses were attached to it, and I measured the water-line marked on his somewhat scanty clothing against the cart. I found that the water was deep enough to wash clean through the foot-board of the vehicle, but hardly deep enough to carry the horses off their legs; so I ordered an immediate inspan, got all my luggage piled on to the seat, on top of which I screwed myself, while my coachman doffed his nether garments. We then made for the drift, having great confidence in the pluck of my little nags. It was ticklish work, for the river was running very strongly; but we pushed through and landed safely on the other bank, when,

E

setting things to rights, we drove on towards Queens-town, to which place we were bound for the Circuit Court.

On arriving there I was warmly greeted by my brother barristers, who told me that a rumour had been circulated that I and the judge—Sir William Hodges—had both been swept away and drowned.

The Chief Justice turned up in the evening all right, having crossed at a still lower drift, terribly frightened, but not a bit hurt.

The day after the Chief Justice's arrival the Circuit Court was held, and some prisoners were charged with gaol-breaking. The judge, who had been to see the prison, which was in a most shameful condition—prisoners huddled together like litters of young pigs, and the place in such a tumbledown condition that it required very little ingenuity to escape from it—said—

"I certainly am not going to punish men for getting away from such a wretched hole as that!"

The result of this remark, and certain comments of the Press, forced the Government to have the old building pulled down and a new prison erected, which I believe is strong, clean, and commodious.

And now for my experience of the worst hailstorm through which I have had to pass. I was on my way to the town or village of Riversdale, and when about five or six miles short of the place I noticed very heavy black clouds coming up behind us. I told my driver to push on as fast as he could, as the storm would soon be upon us. He told me he did not think it would touch us. He was wrong, for in about ten minutes heavy lumps of ice came pelting from the clouds upon us, threatening every moment to batter through the tent of the cart.

The horses, of which I had four—for my wife was with me—at first reared and seemed inclined to bolt, but, apparently changing their minds, suddenly stopped dead short, and, tucking their heads between their forelegs and screwing their tails between the hind ones, thus endured the battering they got.

The pieces of ice which fell around it would be absurd to call hailstones, for they were generally as large as the palm of one's hand, jagged and transparent. They could not have fallen from a very great height, or the consequences would have been more serious than they were. After about half an hour of this pelting it slackened enough to let us go forward on our journey. On arriving at Riversdale we found it a complete scene of desolation. No single pane of glass in the windows of the houses facing the storm was left unsmashed. Gardens were knocked to pieces, young trees split down the centre as if by an axe, and a friend of mine in the place had picked up one of the pieces of ice which would not go into the top of a full-sized tumbler. Many corrugated roofs had been riddled as if by bullet-shots, sheep and poultry killed by the hundred, and the roadways rendered almost impassable by the fall of ice. There was not a quarter of the quantity of glass in the place necessary to supply the damage, and people had to resort to all kinds of contrivances "to expel the winter's wind."

I am afraid that some of my English readers—if I am fortunate enough to have any—will regard my description as one of those "travellers' tales" which no fellow can believe, and yet I have told a true and unvarnished story. An old friend of mine who had at that time been Civil Commissioner and Resident Magistrate of Riversdale was lately seated in the same railway carriage as myself, and I heard him giving an account of this very storm to an acquaintance opposite.

"Do you forget that I was in it?" I asked.

"Oh, of course you were—and your wife, too! I was coming out to meet you both, but the bursting of the storm drove me back and forced me to take refuge in my own house."

This gentleman's narrative entirely corresponded with that which I have just given.

During all the storm there was no thunder or lightning. The reader may ask, How can there be thunder without lightning? I answer, it is quite possible.

I was once travelling in a cart and four with a medical friend from Colesberg to a farm six or seven miles distant. The weather was delicious, and the only signs of anything like a cloud in the heavens were a few of those white fleecy ones which I believe scientific men call *cirrus*. Suddenly a loud peal of thunder rattled above our heads. There was no sign of lightning nor any cloud from which it could have issued. Our horses were greatly frightened, and but for the skill of the coachman in handling them they would have run away. On returning to Colesberg in the afternoon we inquired whether the thunder had been heard there. "Yes, decidedly; and no one could make out what it meant."

Dynamite in the Colony was then unknown; nor

were there any kind of blasting or manufacturing operations going on. I have never been able to account for the phenomenon. Judge Cloete, who was out in the storm I have described, was sitting in the back part of his travelling-waggon when his horses ran away with it, making straight across the *veld* in the direction of a precipice. He laid his hand on the handle of the door so as to spring out if necessity forced him to do so; but the horses in their fright suddenly stopped, and he escaped further danger. His hand, however, was so battered—fortunately it was the left one—that he was forced for some days to wear his arm in a sling. He was then over seventy years of age, but had never in his life witnessed such a storm.

I have witnessed many other hailstorms in the Colony, but nothing like this one. I saw, for instance, the huge Market Square of Kimberley completely covered with hailstones each about the size of the school-boys' marbles, and perfectly white and opaque. In the Riversdale storm, on the other hand, the lumps of ice which fell were, as I have said, jagged in shape and perfectly transparent. The storms in the Cape peninsula seldom bring hailstones much larger than ordinary sugar-plums. I cannot account for the difference.

CHAPTER VIII.

Three Irish Judges—Anecdotes of Judges Fitzpatrick and Dwyer
—Attorney-General Griffith.

THERE have been only three Irishmen who have
been Judges of the Supreme Court in my time.
The first of these was Mr. Justice Fitzpatrick, who
was one of the most pleasant companions and one of
the most genial and witty men I ever knew. I think
I may say he was the only really witty judge we ever
had. I believe he made no pretensions to being
a profound lawyer, but his quickness, keenness of
insight, and knowledge of human nature would have
covered a great many defects if they had existed.

His stories about Ireland were very amusing.
Very many years ago he received the appointment of
Chief Justice of the Gold Coast, and his iron constitution enabled him to withstand the detestable
climate of that country. He used to relate how
friends and companions who accompanied him or
followed him to the country died one by one, leaving
him the sole survivor of the large crew. During his
tenure of this office he had for a time to act as
Governor of the Colony, the actual Governor having
died, or being on leave of absence—I forget which.

One day a deputation of Wesleyans waited upon
him to beg him to make them a grant of some Government land, which they required for the erection of a
church. They were headed by a Wesleyan minister.

This gentleman, thinking, I suppose, to conciliate Mr. Fitzpatrick, who was a Catholic, said to him—

" You see, Governor Fitzpatrick, although I am a Wesleyan you must not suppose that I am a bigot. I have little doubt that I shall meet some good Roman Catholics in Heaven."

" That's provided you manage to get there yourself."

In telling me the story the judge said—

" The coolness of the fellow in assuming that he and his followers were safe to go to Heaven, while it was just possible that two or three poor Roman Catholics might squeeze in through a back gate, rather irritated me, and made me give the rebuff I did. However, I gave them the land, so they went away satisfied."

After enduring the Gold Coast climate for some years, Mr. Fitzpatrick returned to his native country. Later he was made sole Judge of British Kaffraria, then a Crown Colony independent of the Cape, having its own Administrator of Government, its High Court, its Attorney-General, Registrar of Deeds, &c. Mr. Fitzpatrick became very popular, as he could hardly fail to do with his many attractive qualities.

Mr. J——, the Attorney-General, once gave a ball at King William's Town, the capital of the Colony, at which the judge was present. After supper, when a good deal of champagne had been flowing, a well-known merchant of the town sidled up to the judge and said—

" Now, judge, that champagne was not bad—eh ? "

The judge, who told me that he didn't like to depreciate his host's wine, simply said—

" Oh, no ! "

"Well, now," said the merchant, "I put that in to J—— at thirty shillings the dozen."

"Well, then," said the judge, "if I had known that I be hanged if J—— should have put it into me!"

The idea of champagne at thirty shillings a dozen in a country where the price of importation and duties would amount to half that sum, makes one suspect that the wine in question had never seen Reims.

On the annexation of Kaffraria to the Cape Colony Mr. Fitzpatrick was appointed Judge of the Supreme Court, the latter being assigned to the Court of the Eastern Districts held in Grahamstown; and here also he became a favourite with the people. Some years later he took his seat on the Bench of the Supreme Court itself in Cape Town, and there he remained until the illness by which he was invalided, and which led to his death, attacked him. I have already spoken of his geniality, wit, and humour, and I may add that his hospitality equalled his other qualities. , I always had the sincerest regard for him, though in his latter days a scoundrel persuaded him that I had acted as his enemy, in a matter personally affecting him, and I fear that he died in that belief. A more gross and unfounded falsehood than this statement was never made, and it grieves me to think that he died with his mind warped against me by this low fellow, who afterwards died, drunk, outside a common canteen in an up-country village. The judge had no truer or firmer friend than myself.

The second of the three Irish judges was Mr. Justice Dwyer, an M.A. of Trinity College, Dublin, and at first an Irish barrister, but later on he got an *ad eundem* degree at Lincoln's Inn and joined the English Bar. He went the Northern Circuit, and was full of anecdotes about his brother barristers on it. He had not the wit of Mr. Justice Fitzpatrick, but he enjoyed fun very much, and occasionally said humorous things. His first appointment to the Cape was as a Supreme Court judge, but, like Mr. Fitzpatrick, assigned to the Court at Grahamstown.

Travelling once on Circuit in the Eastern Districts, he gave a luncheon party to the Bar and a few other friends, amongst whom was the late Roman Catholic Bishop of Grahamstown, Dr. Ricards. It happened to be a Friday, and the judge, taking his seat at the head of the table, began carving a cold round of beef, and first he handed a plate of it to the Bishop, who quietly passed it on to his neighbours, who were all Protestants. Then afterwards, beginning to help himself to the beef, the Bishop said in expostulatory tones—

"Judge, judge—do you remember that this is Friday?"

"Bless my soul, I had quite forgotten it!" said the judge, putting aside his plate and applying himself to salmon, sardines, and something of that kind. But there was a twinkle about his eye and a slight smile on his lips which attracted the Bishop's notice.

"Now, judge," said he, "you've got some joke— I should like to know what it is?"

"Well," replied the judge, "I was thinking that if we should meet these other fellows in Heaven, what a couple of fools you and I would look!"

The Bishop, who loved a joke as well as any one,

laughed slightly, but of course assumed an air of being a little offended at such a profane joke.

I think the judge rather overrated his own abilities as a lawyer, and he had a quickness of manner which sometimes made him precipitate; but he did his work fairly well. He was a most hospitable man, and his hospitality was well worth enjoying by those who can appreciate a glass of good wine, for his stock was always an excellent one. I was sincerely sorry to lose him when he died, rather unexpectedly, though he had for some time been more or less unwell. He was the youngest-looking man of his age I ever saw, and fond of sport of all kinds.

The third Irish judge was Sir Thomas Upington; but, as I shall have to speak of him further on, I will pass him over for the present.

The Colony has had three Irish Attorney-Generals. The first was Mr. William Porter, a Belfast man, of whom I have already more than once spoken. He was a thoroughly learned lawyer, was sufficiently acquainted with Dutch to use it and quote it, though he always apologised for his pronunciation of it. He also knew French well enough to read it and cite legal authorities in that language; but here, again, he always excused himself for his bad accent. His knowledge of Latin was of course complete, and he pronounced the vowels in the Continental style, which is no doubt infinitely more correct than our own. I have already spoken of his eloquence, which was truly admirable; but besides this, he had an immense capacity for work. As Attorney-General the whole of the criminal cases of the Colony had to pass through his hands; but he performed the work perfectly, with no other assistance than that of one chief and one assistant clerk, and it seemed to cost him no particular effort.

Mr. Denyssen, on the contrary, who acted for him during Mr. Porter's six months' absence in Europe, protested to me that the work was killing him. Of Mr. Porter's almost unbounded munificence it is almost superfluous to speak to those who had any knowledge of him. By his will he left £30,000 to form a reformatory for young lads who had been convicted of offences. His private charities were innumerable, but he concealed them as carefully as possible—

> "He was a man—take him for all in all,
> We shall not look upon his like again."

The next Irish Attorney-General was Mr. William Downes Griffith, who succeeded Mr. Porter on the retirement of the latter on pension. Mr. Griffith was a totally different man from his predecessor, but he had a strong character of his own. He was an M.A. of Trinity College, Dublin, and, besides his classical and mathematical attainments, he was a man of science, his special hobby being chemistry, of which he had made a particular study as a "special study," as required by his University. Originally he was intended for the Irish Bar; but his destiny was afterwards changed, and he was called to the English Bar in the Inner Temple. He was literally saturated with law; but it had not spoilt his classical, literary, and artistic tastes. He was born in Dublin, and was a thorough Irishman in the best sense of the word. To say that he was popular in this Colony would be to pervert the truth. Few men made a greater number of enemies. I think this was the consequence partly of his thorough independence of character, and partly of the somewhat disagreeable manner in which he occasionally manifested it. But he had a knot of staunch friends—amongst whom I think I may reckon myself—who admired him greatly, and liked him for the excellent social qualities he possessed.

He had a great dislike for any man whom he considered a sneak or dishonest. His very soul revolted against people of that class. He was apt to be a little hot-tempered—he is still alive, but will forgive me for saying this. He had a great friend in a barrister named John Cyprian Thompson—now, alas! dead—and they used to correspond together in doggerel Latin. I had the privilege of seeing most of the letters, which were immensely funny. Mr. Thompson always addressed Mr. Griffith as "Care Bedaddi," declaring that whenever Griffith got excited he always came out with the word "bedad." Thompson's letters were often illustrated with perfect little gems of pen-and-ink comic sketches in the margin.

When it was proposed to introduce a Bill into our Parliament to establish responsible government, Mr. Griffith flatly refused to take charge of the Bill, believing that the Colony was quite unfit for the proposed change. He therefore obtained leave of absence for a time. Meantime Mr. Jacobs, who was the Solicitor-General in Grahamstown, was sent for to act in his stead. The Bill was carried and responsible government established. Upon this Mr. Griffith retired altogether on a fairly good pension, which, however, he has seldom drawn, having shortly after

his retirement from the Colony been appointed by
the Lord Chancellor one of the County Court Judges
in England; and our Civil Service regulations do not
allow any one who has obtained a Government
appointment in any part of the British Dominions to
draw his Colonial pension as well as his pay, unless
the latter should in amount be less than the pension,
in which case he is entitled to the difference between
the two. Mr. Griffith is still alive, and nobody
wishes him more sincerely than I do all health and
prosperity.

The third Irish Attorney-General was, and now is,
Sir Thomas Upington. He has been popular in his
office, the duties of which he has performed with the
greatest ability. But I am not going to speak of
him fully at present, as I shall have occasion to do so
in a future chapter.

When I first commenced practice there was no
Attorney-General for the whole Colony. Now the
office may be said to be divided: there is a Solicitor-
General for the Eastern Districts, having jurisdiction
over them only and stationed at Grahamstown.
There is also a Crown Prosecutor of Griqualand
stationed at Kimberley, his duties and jurisdiction
being confined to the territory of Griqualand. Over
both these offices, however, the Attorney-General
possesses paramount authority, of which, however, he
very seldom takes advantage. The increase of the
population of the Colony makes these three officers
necessary, and gives them plenty of work to occupy
their time.

CHAPTER IX.

Antagonism of Races—Gross Exaggeration—Cape Ladies—Cape
Servants.

A GREAT deal has been talked and written lately about the antagonism between the Dutch and English races here—the English papers especially seem to be never tired of the theme. My all but forty-seven years' experience of this Colony, during which I have visited nearly every district of it, leads me to regard all this talk as fallacious. I do not mean to say that no antagonism exists, but I believe it to be almost entirely confined to the lowest class of each nationality. Thus we constantly hear of the most ignorant class of Dutch Boers talking about the "*verdomde*" Englishman; and, on the other hand, many of the lower classes of English origin are apt to express their contempt of "those d——d Dutchmen." No one in the better classes takes any notice or attaches any importance to this vulgar dislike. Among the more cultivated classes of each race the feeling is next to non-existent. Many of the better-born of the Colonists of Dutch origin are as well educated and cultivated as their English fellow Colonists—indeed, a great number of them have received their education almost entirely in England or Scotland. Many of them have pedigrees of which even Englishmen would be proud; for it is not many men who can trace their ancestry to two

hundred and fifty years, which some of the Cape
Dutch families do. They have imbibed a taste for
all English sports and amusements—delight in horse-
racing, are skilful at cricket, and can give a very good
account of themselves in the hunting-field or in the
ball-room.

They are generally good speakers, and display their
abilities in this direction in our local Houses of Parliament. And then the intermarriage of the two
races is so common that it would be difficult to say
of the Colonist if he has more English or Dutch
blood in his veins.

The ladies of Dutch origin born and bred in this
Colony are, as a rule, cultivated women of good taste,
and, like the men, pursue all the English amusements suitable to their sex. No more excellent
mothers, I believe, exist. There is no doubt, however, that occasionally a little soreness exists from
the idea that imported Englishmen are apt to depreciate Cape-born ladies. I can give an instance of this.

Many years ago, when I was editing the 'Cape
Monthly Magazine,' an article appeared in it entitled
"The Flagship Ball." It was in fact an account of
a ball given in Simon's Bay by the Admiral of the
station on board the ship which carried his flag.
The article was very amusing and vivacious, but
contained a few sarcastic remarks on the dress and
manners of a few—not by any means all—of the
Cape young ladies present. This gave offence in
many quarters, and the author received plenty of
abuse; amongst others, the editor of a Grahamstown newspaper spoke of the writer as one of those
flippant gentlemen from England who sneer at every-

thing Colonial, and especially at Cape-born ladies, though, it added, they sometimes don't object to marry them. This was, of course, intended for myself, and alluded to the fact that I had married a lady of Cape birth. The fun of the thing was that I was not the writer at all, but the article was the production of an English-born young lady, clever and lively, who had not a single relation or connection of any kind in the Colony—in fact, one of the daughters of the Admiral himself.

I think a well-born, well-educated girl of Dutch origin one of the most charming people in the world, with plenty of sense and perfect self-possession. Lord Byron thus describes a young English *débutante* of his day—

> " 'Tis true your budding miss is very charming,
>   But shy and awkward at first coming out,
> So much alarmed that she is quite alarming,
>   All giggle, blush, half pertinence, half pout—
> And glancing at mamma for fear there's harm in
>   What you, she, it, or they may be about.
> The nursery still peeps out in all they utter—
> And then they always smell of bread-and-butter."

Now, this would be a grossly unfair description of a well-bred Cape young lady making her first appearance in society. She would exhibit no shyness nor awkwardness; would certainly not think of looking to mamma, but take all the attentions paid her gracefully; and, as a matter of course, throw herself into the enjoyment of the pleasures prepared for her. She generally rides well, dresses well, and occasionally sings well; is an adept at lawn-tennis, and manages a bicycle as well as her English sisters. She is far from deficient in education or general accomplishments. Take her for all in all, she is a charming, straightforward, energetic specimen of womanhood—

> "A simple woman, not too good
> For human nature's daily food."

But good enough for that at any rate. It must not be supposed, however, that there are no exceptions to the picture I have drawn. On the contrary, I must confess that I have seen many ill-bred Cape young ladies, who fancied themselves attractive when they were only impertinent, and believed in the admiration of the very men who were laughing at them in their sleeves.

English and Dutch servants—the latter mostly coloured—do not pull very well together. It must be confessed that the female coloured servant of the Colony is generally an unpleasant sluggard, doing her work in a most careless manner, causing her mistress many a sigh over broken glass and crockery, and spoiling the dishes she pretends to cook. English servants, on the other hand, are apt to form a little too high opinion of themselves, and to demand wages about double the amount of what they would have earned at home. Then they are very keen on getting married; so that when a mistress thinks that she has pretty well trained a girl to suit her ways, she gets the announcement that Mary Jane is going to be married. With, of course, a great many exceptions, I think that both classes of servants may be pronounced to be fairly honest, and some are in this respect beyond praise.

F

Men-servants in the Colony are of two classes—
coloured and white.   Of the coloured there are
several different races—Kaffirs, Hottentots, Basutos,
Malays, and others.   They are almost the sole
agricultural labourers in the Colony, and this is
easily accounted for.   An Englishman would never
consent to sit all day in the broiling sun to herd
sheep or cattle, nor would he be equal to cope with
ordinary agricultural labour in such a climate as
ours.   The wages, too, are infinitely less in the
case of the coloured man than would satisfy an
Englishman.   A few of these coloured races make
very fair cooks and house-servants generally, while
the Malays are renowned as coachmen, and can
handle a team of eight or ten horses as easily as an
English driver would manage his four-in-hand.
Strangers are generally surprised at the skill ex-
hibited by these Malay coachmen.   English male
servants are not often found, except in the houses of
the richer classes, as family coachmen or grooms.
Like many other countries, the Cape often cries out
about its want of good servants ; but from all I read
and hear, the complaints are just as loud on the subject in England.   Altogether, I fancy it is not so
very much worse off in this respect than the Mother
Country.   I may add that many of the coloured
people, especially the Malays, make excellent arti-
ficers, brick and stone masons, carpenters, wheel-
wrights, &c. ; while some are profitably engaged in
trade on their own account.   They are all very fond
of holidays, especially the Malays, who take Friday
as their so-called Sabbath, Saturday, which is a half-
holiday all over the country, Sunday as a matter of
course, and Monday, which they generally appro-

priate to picnics and other amusements. Altogether it may be said that it is seldom that a Malay man works more than four days out of the seven.

It must be borne in mind that what I have said with regard to the supposed antagonism between the Dutch and English races has nothing whatever to do with other States and Colonies in South Africa, and especially they could not apply to the people of the Transvaal Republic : there race hatred has been cultivated to an extreme extent. This is accounted for by the petting and fondling with which the Government of the Republic has treated the Boers and the Hollanders there, making these people fancy that they are not only lords of the soil, but the only persons fit to govern the country, and to treat the English inhabitants of the same State, whose capital and industry have made the country rich and prosperous, and who pay about three-fourths of the taxes, as quite unentitled to take any part in the Government—not even so far as to have a vote for the members of the Legislature.

This condition of affairs cannot last long ; the Dutchmen are overbearing and insolent, the Englishmen savagely indignant. Either matters will have to be arranged—and that very shortly—by firmness on the part of the British Government, and a little sensible concession on the part of the Republic, or they will produce a state of war and bloodshed horrible to contemplate. For these results we are indebted first to Mr. Gladstone, and secondly to Oom Paul Kruger—probably the two most wrong-headed and perverse-minded men the present century has seen.

CHAPTER X.

Travelling generally—Upset with a Rev. D.D.—A Prayer-
Meeting and Harmony.

In the early part of this volume I spoke of the
manner in which Cape barristers travel on Circuit.
I may now make a few remarks on travelling in
general in the Colony. Away from lines of railway,
which are unfortunately very limited in comparison
with the huge extent of our country, journeying is
usually done either by waggon or Cape cart. Both
these vehicles have of late years been frequently
described, so that I need not trouble my readers with
any fresh account of them. I may say, however,
that I think the Cape cart a wonderful vehicle. It
is on two wheels, and has only two, or sometimes
three, seats or benches, and yet it is quite a common
sight, especially on Saint Monday, to see eight, ten,
or even twelve people crammed into one on the
road between Cape Town and Kalk Bay. They are
chiefly Malays, bound to a picnic or some other
excursion. They are very happy; but Malays as a
rule do not make much noise over their enjoyments,
being, like other Moslems, rather reserved in tone.
They do, however, indulge in songs; and I pity the
people who hear them, for Malay music is a thing of
itself, and I hope it will remain so.

A Cape cart is an admirable travelling vehicle,
light, strong, and going easily over the broken roads,

which are somewhat plentiful in the Colony. It is astonishing what a quantity of baggage and provisions you can pack into them, which, like the proverbial carpet-bag, is never full.

I have also spoken of post-carts in the country. On one occasion, having been detained in Cape Town by a domestic event for about a month after my brother barristers had started on Circuit, I determined to join them by taking rather out-of-the-way routes. First, I took the post-cart to Beaufort West; there, after a halt for breakfast and changing horses, I started again in the same cart; but this time I had two fellow-passengers, one of them a Rev. D.D. of the Dutch Reformed Church, who took his seat by my side at the back of the cart, and we started in the usual post-cart style—that is, at full gallop. The reverend Doctor got rather nervous.

"I hope, Mr. Cole," he said, "this man won't upset us."

"It is as likely as not," I said, "for he is as drunk as a fiddler; I noticed it just as we were starting. But, Doctor," I said, laughing, "if he does capsize us, I hope it will be on your side, so that I may have something soft to fall on." The Doctor was very plump indeed, and I then rather slender.

I had scarcely said the words before the man drove against an ant-hill by the roadside, and upset the cart completely bottom upwards. I did fall on the Doctor, and heard his grunt as I did so. We had some little difficulty in extricating our legs from the mass of letter-bags and luggage with which the cart had been loaded. When we got upon our legs the Doctor said to me—

" Mr. Cole, I don't intend to go on any further in this cart—do you ? "

I answered, " Certainly not," and I suggested that one of us should go back to Beaufort West, only about two miles away, and hire a cart, while the other should remain in charge of the luggage by the roadside.   I volunteered to go myself; but the Doctor would not allow me, as he said he knew the place better than I did, and would be able more readily to find a cart; so I sat down on our *impedimenta* waiting for the Doctor's return.   He arrived shortly in a cart, into which we placed our luggage and ourselves, and drove back to the village.   Here, after an hour or so, I managed to purchase a cart and pair, paying, of course, at least half as much again as they were worth.   Then the Doctor and I side by side made a fresh start.

Late in the afternoon we were met by another reverend gentleman, a cousin and namesake of my friend; all three of us then went on our way to a farmhouse where the other two were expected, and where we were to pass the night.   Nothing could exceed the cordiality with which we were received, for the hospitality was equally extended to myself as the others.   We had a dinner—or, rather, supper—the table being loaded with turkeys and poultry of all kinds, to say nothing of sweet dishes, of which the housewife seemed to be proud.   After supper we had what is called a prayer-meeting, the services being, of course, in the Dutch language, which I scarcely understood sufficiently to follow all that was said. Then, again, there was a great singing of hymns, in which the voices were more powerful than the music chaste. The little old grandmother of the family, who sat at a small table by herself at the corner of the room, was especially loud and shrill. After all this was over we were shown into a bedroom which we had to share. There were two beds in it, and the clergymen insisted on my taking one of them while they shared the other. At early daybreak we started again, our kind hosts refusing to accept a penny from either of us either for food or forage.

Going along the road my friend the reverend Doctor asked me whether I had ever been at one of these prayer-meetings before. I replied that I had not.

"And may I ask what you thought of it?" he pursued.

"Well, Doctor, perhaps you might be annoyed if I told you."

"Oh no—there's no fear of that!"

"Well, to tell you the truth, Doctor, I was thinking how the cherubs and seraphs would be scared when the old lady took her voice aloft and let free amongst them."

The Doctor tried to look grave, but hardly succeeded, for he burst out laughing.

At a certain village further on, whither they were bound, I parted with my two friends and went on alone. I had to make particular inquiries about the cross-road I was to take and the accommodation I was to find for the night. I received full directions, and was told that at about sundown I should come upon a large farmhouse on a property belonging to a Mr. Van de Merwe, and called "Zeekoe Vley." The Van der Merwes, I was told, were better educated and more civilized than the generality of Dutch farmers, but that "they hated the sight of an Englishman." I took very little notice of this, as I had so often heard the same words spoken and yet found the people to whom they were applied kind and hospitable. I knew also that the farmers generally liked advocates, and are especially civil to them— probably thinking they may require their assistance some day, as they are somewhat inclined to litigation.

At sundown I reached a large house, which I recognised from the description I had received of it as Mr. Van de Merwe's. A fine, tall young fellow was walking up and down the street. Pulling up, I got down, and, raising my hat, I asked him, in the best Dutch I could command, whether I might outspan there. The young man at once gave me permission, asking me who I was. I told him I was Advocate Cole.

"Oh!" he said, "I know Mynheer's name well, although I have never seen him before."

I asked if I could get some forage, and was told, "Certainly;" and whether I could stay there for the night, and was again answered, "Certainly." He then called to one of his men to come and assist my servant in taking out the horses and leading them to the stable. He then asked me to come into the house, and as soon as we had entered he apologised to me for the absence of his father, who he said was away on a journey, and for his mother, who was sick, while his only sister was attending on her. We sat down, and I began airing my bad Dutch, until at last I wondered to myself whether I could find anything further to say in that language. Suddenly a bright idea struck me.

"Perhaps," I said in my own tongue, "Mynheer speaks English?"

"Oh, yes," he replied, "I speak English—speaking it just as well as I can. I was brought up at an English school at Uitenhage, and I received all my education in that language."

"Then why on earth didn't you tell me that before?" I exclaimed.

"Well, I wished to see how you would get on."

The fact is he had been "pulling my leg" all the while; but I was so pleased at the process being concluded that I made no complaints. We then had a chat together, and struck up quite a friendship.

After a time he conducted me to the dining-room, where we had an excellent supper; and I sent to my cart for a bottle of Bass and one of sherry, and with these and some cigars I had with me we passed the evening pleasantly enough.

I told him a number of stories, some of which might have been rather stale in Cape Town, but were new to him living in such an out-of-the-way place. He enjoyed them heartily, and contributed a few of his own about neighbours and various mishaps at shooting, hunting, &c. Then he led me to my bedroom, where, on one of the big soft feather beds for which the Dutch farm-houses are famous, I slept as soundly as I ever did in my life. At peep of day I got up, and found my friend already risen with a cup of excellent coffee ready for me, my cart inspanned ready for a start. He had also entrusted some provisions to my servant for the road. Before parting I asked him what I owed him, and the reply was, "Nothing."

" But," I. said, " surely for the forage," because I knew that most farmers, while refusing to accept any money in return for the food and lodging they give you, accept payment for the forage you have had ; and they are quite right, for forage is part of their stock-in-trade, part of the produce of their farm—in fact, by the sale of which they live. But my friend persistently refused to take a penny, saying that he had never enjoyed an evening in his life as yesterday, and expressing his earnest wish that I should come back to him some day. But his place was so far out of the way of our Circuit route that I never saw it or him again ; but I have never forgotten the cordial reception I had from one who formed part of the family that " hated the very sight of an Englishman."

I was once travelling with my wife on our road to Graaff Reinet, having with us a newly-married young lady to whom my wife had given a seat in the cart. In the evening we drew up at a house where we were expected—the house was the property of Mr. Lotz, one of the richest men in the district, owning thousands of acres of land, on one border of which rose a mountain to which his name had been given—Lotzberg. Our host came out and greeted us most cordially, conducting us and the rest of the Circuit party into the house, which was a large well-built one with polished teak floors, window-sashes, and doors, and furnished in quite European fashion.

Having shown the bachelor portion of the party to a room destined for their occupation that night, he led my wife and Mrs. E.—to whom we had been introduced—and myself into a fine large room containing a couple of handsome four-post brass bedsteads with lace curtains and hangings.

"This," he said, "is for Mr. and Mrs. Cole and Mrs. E."

Whereat the little lady raised her eyes in astonishment; which, however, was vastly increased by my wife, who was very fond of fun, who with a hurried glance towards me said—

"Oh, thank you, Mr. Lotz—that will be very comfortable!"—and, turning to Mrs. E., she went on —"You see, you can have that bedstead to yourself, and we will take this one, and my husband can undress behind the curtains, and so it will be all right."

The poor little woman looked positively aghast to think an English lady should sanction such a dreadful arrangement. I believe she felt inclined to rush out of the house and hide herself in the bushes.

I suppose I need scarcely tell my readers that after we had all had a good supper and it became time to go to rest, I followed the bachelors into their room, leaving the two ladies in possession of the other one with the brass bedsteads. When our host heard this in the morning he was thoroughly surprised, and could not conceive what fault we could find in the arrangements he had made for us. Saying, I daresay, to himself, "What queer notions some of these English have!" But his farewell to us was as kindly and cordial as had been his reception to us the previous evening.

CHAPTER XI.

Libel and Slander—Duelling—My own Experiences—Fighting a Lady.

ACTIONS for libel or slander are far from being uncommon in this country. They are brought not only in the Supreme and Circuit, but they are brought also in the Magistrates' Court. I am sorry to say that very often the words complained of are spoken by a woman, and her husband has to pay the penalty. These suits are very expensive when brought in the higher Courts, for there is generally a great conflict of evidence in them, and the damages given are sometimes what is called "exemplary." But a great many of these actions are settled by apologies, and some of the apologies are so degradingly mean that it seems impossible they could be signed by people having the slightest trace of manliness in them. It is no unusual thing to find one of them couched in somewhat such terms as these :—

"I hereby confess that the words I uttered reflecting on the character of Mr. B. are totally without foundation ; that I know nothing whatever against him, but believe him to be a most honourable gentleman. I confess myself to be a wicked liar, and I thank Mr. B. for letting me off with this apology, which I have authorised him to publish in such newspapers as he may select."

Such productions as these almost make us wish for the return of the old days of duelling, when a man who slandered another put his own life in danger. But no, I am glad that duelling has died out in this Colony as completely as it has done in England, being killed there mostly by ridicule.

On the European continent the practice still prevails. In France they are generally mere farces. Two men cross rapiers, and one pinks the other slightly in the arm, inflicting a wound which scarcely requires more than a bit of sticking-plaster to heal it, and then they are satisfied. It is strange that the most quick-witted and sensitive nation in Europe should fail to see the ludicrous light in which these duels place their citizens. In Germany duels are often savage and sometimes brutal, and much the same is the case in Russia. The Italians seldom fight duels, the rule being for the injured man to stick a stiletto into the back of his traducer—a convenient plan, saving much time and trouble.

I myself have never fought a duel or been challenged to do so, but I have had two somewhat different experiences connected with them. The first was in Port Elizabeth, when I was a very young man. One of my greatest friends there was a Lieutenant D——, commanding a detachment of the 27th Regiment, quartered in the town. A young gentleman whom I will call R—— greatly cultivated D——'s society, seldom failing to call on him daily. He was an amiable youth, but very feather-headed, and D—— was very fond of teasing. One day he went to D——'s hotel, and going upstairs into his room began—

" Well, D——, old fellow, how are you to-day ? "

D—— assumed a look of blank amazement, saying—
"And pray sir, who are you?"

"Oh, come, old fellow, don't play the fool like that!" said R——.

D——, still preserving his gravity, rang the bell, and a waiter appeared.

. "Waiter," said D——, "pray, who *is* this gentleman? Can you tell me?"

The waiter, who had so constantly seen them together, put on a broad grin.

"Oh, well," said R——, in a rage, "if you mean to insult me you shall hear from me!"—and he stalked out of the room and out of the house.

An hour or so later a gentleman, who announced himself as a friend of R——'s, called upon D——, and said he was commissioned by his friend to demand satisfaction for the insult D—— had put upon him.

"Oh, it's a challenge," said D——. "I must refer you to my friend Mr. Cole—do you know him?"

He did know me, and shortly afterwards called upon me. After a little talk we arranged our plans, and a meeting was fixed to take place next morning in a valley close to Port Elizabeth.

At the appointed hour the two principals and the two seconds appeared upon the ground. We—the seconds—handed to each opponent a formidable looking duelling-pistol, which we had carefully loaded with blank cartridge only. The proper distance was measured off, the two antagonists were set facing each other, and at the given signal both fired. D——, who was in the secret, fell flat on the ground as if mortally wounded; while R——, throwing down his pistol, cried—"Heavens, I have killed my dearest friend!"

and rushed to D——'s prostrate form. D——, putting his thumb to his nose and extending his fingers, took "a sight" at R——, who was so enraged at this that he wanted to insist on a genuine duel *à outrance;* but we seconds interfered, and after a little palaver persuaded him to accept the whole affair as a practical joke from beginning to end; and then the four of us returned to Port Elizabeth and cracked a bottle of champagne over the event.

My second experience bid first to be a more serious one. A group of young barristers and students were chatting together in Inner Temple Lane. Among the barristers was a Mr. D——y S——r, and one E—— G——. S—— in the course of the talk said something which was considered very insulting to G——, and, having said the words, walked away to his chambers.

"He has insulted me!" cried G—— in a rage.

"Challenge him—challenge him!" cried some of the young fellows.

"Be jabers, I will then! Cole, will you act for me?"

I, who in those days dearly loved fun and mischief, walked down to S——'s chambers, found him there, and stated my errand. S—— was inclined to treat the affair with ridicule; but I assured him the matter was serious.

"Why, you know," said S——, "if I accepted the challenge your friend would never fight."

"Then, by Jove," I added hotly, "I give you my word of honour I will fight for him!"

S—— looked grave, and I began again to point out to him that his language had really been insulting, and in the end induced him to authorise me to convey his apologies to G——. I am not imputing cowardice to S————, for I daresay he was greatly influenced by the reflection that it would be somewhat ridiculous to "go out" on such a trumpery affair.

General Cloete, whom I have mentioned in a former chapter, did actually fight a duel in the outskirts of Cape Town, where he then held the office of Colonel Commandant. He had made some remarks reflecting on the effeminate voice and appearance of Dr. Barry, then principal medical officer of the troops in garrison, and the Doctor at once challenged him to mortal combat. The meeting took place on the Flats, near Cape Town, and shots were exchanged, but without effect. The seconds then intervened, and insisted that there should be no more fighting. The parties were induced to shake hands, and all returned together to Cape Town.

It was fortunate for the Colonel that he did not hit his antagonist, for after death it was discovered that Dr. Barry was a woman who had successfully disguised her sex all her life. She had passed the London hospitals, taken high degrees and medical diplomas, joined the forces as army surgeon, and in that capacity gained great reputation and fame for ability. It is said that only one man in the world knew the secret of her sex, and he, of course, never divulged it. This was Lord Charles Somerset, then Governor of the Cape Colony.

CHAPTER XII.

The Law of the Colony and the Law of England.

IT is scarcely necessary to tell even my English readers that the law of the Cape of Good Hope is the Roman-Dutch—that is, the law of Holland based principally on the Roman. I am not going to write a disquisition on it; it would not interest non-professionals, while those with legal knowledge would probably refer to the proverb about the grand-mother and her eggs. But I may say that I greatly admire it, and believe that no other system is better capable of rendering justice between man and man. As a matter of course we have borrowed consider-ably from the law of England, especially in criminal and mercantile cases. It must be remembered that the latest commentators on the Roman-Dutch law, as taken over in this country—Van der Linden and Van der Keessel—wrote no later than the commence-ment of the present century. At that time by the criminal law of Holland, like that of England, men were hanged for stealing a single sheep, or less matters than that, while some punishments were cruel in the extreme. The various reforms in the English Criminal Code have been effected from time to time almost, I might say, to the present day. The Roman-Dutch law has long been superseded in

G

Holland by the Code Napoleon, and consequently has remained unchanged. The criminal law as now administered in this Colony is almost identical with that of England. In mercantile cases, too, it has been necessary to move forward with the times, for to quote decisions of one hundred years ago in commercial transactions would be palpably absurd, except so far as such decisions laid down certain broad principles which could not be lost sight of.

The law is administered in the Colony, first, by the Supreme Court and its two branches, Grahamstown and Kimberley.

Secondly, by the Circuit Courts, which are held twice a year in each district of the country, and these Courts have within the district in which they are held the same power as the Supreme Court.

Thirdly, there are the Magistrates' Courts, one being established in every division of the Colony.

The jurisdiction of these last is naturally restricted both in criminal and civil cases. In the higher Courts criminal cases are tried before a judge and a jury of nine men, whose verdict, as in England, must be unanimous. In civil cases trial by jury in the Supreme Court may take place if the parties to the suit so desire, but it is very rarely that a jury is asked for.

I have said that we have borrowed considerably from the law of England, and I think that the latter might with advantage borrow from our law in certain cases, say, for instance, lunacy and divorce. The English process in the former is very prolix, and I am afraid sometimes slightly muddles the judges; while in the latter the relief of the dissolution of the marriage is granted only for the cause of infidelity; we have a second cause, namely, " malicious desertion," which to me seems as good a cause as the other. But I must not discuss this subject, lest I should call down the thunders of the Church upon my head.

The magistrates of the Colony are as a body well-educated and highly conscientious. Some of them have had legal training, or have applied themselves assiduously to the study of the law, and, of course, these make the most efficient magistrates. The others, having little or no training in the law, have to trust mainly to their own common sense, which, however, is by no means a safe guide, for A.'s common sense may lead him to quite a different conclusion that B.'s might do. That they all desire to do justice to the best of their ability is to my mind clear. They make mistakes now and then, but seldom very serious ones, and there are comparatively few appeals from their judgments.

I shall give two or three instances more or less amusing of some of their decisions: the first shows great quickness and knowledge of human nature on the magistrate's part.

A loafing sot was charged before him for about the twentieth time for being drunk and incapable. The case was quickly proved, and the magistrate told the prisoner that he must give him one month's hard labour, at which the man looked almost pleased. But, said the magistrate, turning to the gaoler, " take care that this man is well scrubbed from head to foot with soap-and-water every day that he remains in gaol." The prisoner's face betrayed the utmost con-

G 2

sternation.   At the end of the month, when he was
released, he made his way as quickly as possible out
of the village and district, and was never seen in
either again.

The next instance shows curious ignorance on
the part of a certain occupant of the magisterial
bench.   The case was tried before him, in the course
of which the agent for the plaintiff quoted a passage
from Van der Linden.   It so happened that the
name of the Dutch Reformed Minister of the place
was Van der Lingen.

Says the magistrate—

"I know Mr. Van der Lingen very well; he is a
very good man and a very good minister, but he has
nothing to say in this Court."

He had evidently never heard of the great Dutch
jurist.

The third instance is of a very different kind to
the other two.   Very many years ago an old gentleman was made magistrate of Simon's Town.   A suit
was brought in his Court in which the plaintiff sued
for the restoration of a horse, which he said was his
property, but was unlawfully detained by the defendant.   At the trial the plaintiff produced a crowd of
witnesses, who all swore that they knew the horse
quite well, and that it was certainly the property of
the plaintiff.

The defendant, on the other hand, produced an
equally large crowd of witnesses, who swore point-
blank that they also knew the horse, and it clearly
belonged to the defendant.   It was, in short, a case
of conflict of evidence, through which a practised
advocate might have found it difficult to have made

his way. The magistrate looked puzzled; then, addressing the plaintiff, said—

"You don't know a bit whether the horse is yours or not."

And then to the defendant—

"And you don't know whether the horse is yours, either, and you come here and want me to find out which of you it belongs to. I tell you what it is— I'll see you both d——d first!"

The clerk of the Court discreetly entered this on the roll as absolution from the instance, each party paying his own costs; and this was really about what the magistrate meant; but he was an old sailor, and expressed his judgment in somewhat unconventional terms.

A few more words with regard to our magistrates. Nearly every one of them is also Civil Commissioner of his district, his principal duties being to collect its revenues—mostly quit-rents—and to issue stamps, receive transfer dues, and so forth. He is also expected to make himself thoroughly acquainted, not only with the boundaries of his own division, but of those of most of the farms within it; and he is President of the Divisional Council, and he has charge of the roads.

It will be seen that these duties have no natural connection with those of a magistrate, and a man may be a very good officer in one capacity and anything but a good one in the other. Considering that the magistrates are selected from all branches of the Civil Service, one can imagine a custom-house or post-office clerk making a capital Civil Commissioner, but, from never having opened a law-book, a very poor magistrate. It has always seemed to me that the two offices should be kept distinct, as is the case with the division of the Cape and that of Griqualand West. Some attempts have been made within the last three or four years to establish examinations in law among Civil servants, the successful candidates being supposed to have a preferable claim to be appointed to vacant magistracies. However, these examinations are, to use a well-worn phrase, "a step in the right direction."

CHAPTER XIII.

Climate and Scenery.

NOT very long ago one of the most distinguished members of our House of Assembly spoke of our "unequalled climate." With all deference to the honourable gentleman, I must say that this is nonsense. The Colony has not one climate only, but at least four or five different ones. To begin with, there is the climate of the Cape peninsula, as we call that part of the Colony beginning with the shores of Table Mountain and ending at Cape Point, which is the Cape of Good Hope proper. A somewhat distinguished visitor from England lately eulogised the beautiful and varied scenery of this part of the Colony, but said he thought the climate detestable. Without going so far as this, I may say that I think it is anything but an agreeable one. The winters are cold and damp, with downfalls of rain lasting often four, five, or six days together, with an interval now and then of a wretched drizzle, making one's body feel, as Mr. Mantalini says, "a dem'd moist unpleasant one," with a variety now and then in the shape of thunderstorms. The gales that set into Table Bay at this season used, before the completion of the breakwater, to play havoc with the shipping. In summer we have our far-famed south-easters, than which it is difficult to imagine a more disagreeable wind. It whirls up clouds of dust and sand, blows down young trees and sometimes old ones, unroofs a few houses, and renders it difficult for even strong and active people to keep their legs, while in the meantime they are being choked. It makes Table Bay a sheet of white foam, and vessels can rarely anchor or leave it while its fury lasts, and it often does last for many days together. When it ceases the heat is generally intense, and of that moist kind which is generally more oppressive than heat of a dry atmosphere.

It must not be supposed that I mean to say we have no really fine weather; indeed, we have some of the most beautiful weather in the world, and this for a time makes us forget south-easters in the one season and rain-storms in the other. I have said nothing about spring or autumn, because they hardly exist except in name—generally we plunge headlong from winter into summer, and from summer into winter. The early summer has generally some cold, and the early winter some hot, days. As a curious specimen of weather, I may refer to the last summer (1895), when we had to use house-fires to within two days of Christmas Day, which would be about the same thing as using them up to the 22nd of June.

Then there is the climate of the coast-line country, extending along the shores of the Indian Ocean as far as East London. The climate of this line of country is somewhat similar to that of the Cape peninsula, but is less subject to sudden and violent changes. It is also occasionally afflicted with droughts, which seldom affect us, and enjoys a great many more thunderstorms than we do. Beyond East London and the Transkei comes Pondoland, of which

I know nothing personally; but an excellent authority, Mr. R. W. Murray, Junr., who has lived a great deal in it, says that, taking the climate all the year round, it is the most delicious one he has ever lived in.

Then we have the great Karroo—a vast tract of sun-baked clay, with scarcely any vegetation beyond a little stunted bush, generally not more than a foot high. It is difficult to imagine a drier climate than this. I have been on farms in the Karroo where not a drop of rain has fallen for two whole consecutive years. This gives it the reputation of being very beneficial to invalids suffering from pulmonic complaints; and I believe it is so, but that scarcely makes it a pleasant climate for healthy people to live in. The winters are generally cold and the summers occasionally desperately hot, and yet the soil of this barren tract, with plenty of water supplied to it, becomes one of the most fertile in the world. I have often visited a farm in the Karroo called " Zoutkloof," which has an unfailing spring of water upon it, and I have never seen finer figs or potatoes, besides many other kinds of fruit and vegetables, than are grown in the garden of this place. I may add that attempts have of late been made to raise water to the surface of the soil by means of artesian wells, and many of these attempts have proved very successful. If the success should continue over great tracts of land, the appearance of the country would become wholly changed and the climate vastly improved.

Then there is Griqualand West, which is, strictly speaking, a part of the Karroo country, but the climate very different. In winter the nights and early mornings are frequently frosty, and pools of water covered with thin ice; during the greater portion of the day the air is deliciously fresh, cool, and bracing, so that merely to breathe it seems to make life worth living. There is something approaching to spring and autumn there, but of very short duration. The summer is very hot, but perfectly dry heat, making it by no means oppressive, as you would anticipate from the thermometer. I have sat on the Bench of the High Court for two or three consecutive days with the thermometer from 100° to 107° in the shade, and yet I have suffered less inconvenience than I have experienced with the thermometer only a little over 80°. The ugliest part of the summer is the prevalence of dust-storms; they beat even our south-easters in force, breaking down trees, lifting roofs off houses, and depositing them where they were never intended to be, and making it almost impossible to leave your house while they continue. Fortunately they are generally of only short duration—say two hours or so, and mostly followed by thunderstorms and heavy rain. In the early days of the Diamond Fields there was a great deal of what was called "camp fever"; but with the magnificent supply of water which the town of Kimberley now has, the better-constructed dwellings, and the cleanlier habits of life, I look upon Kimberley as a healthy town—at all events, I spent about four or five years there without an hour's illness.

I have already spoken of the Great Karroo and its climate, but it is beaten in regard to this by Nama-qualand—a waterless land, as its name implies.

Droughts are so long and so frequent in that country that, as is the case at this moment, they spread famine and distress through the land. At the same time a part of this country is rich in minerals, especially in copper, the mines of which are pretty well known everywhere, and, I may add, is fortunate in being well represented in Parliament.

But I have, so far, omitted another tract of country, namely the uplands of Albany, Queenstown, and other districts. These have a very good climate, reversing the order of things in the Cape peninsula; they get nearly all their rain in summer principally by thunder-storms, while the winters are cold, dry, and bracing; and they are justly considered very healthy districts.

Now I leave my readers to judge whether I was not correct in saying that the Cape has not one climate, but about half-a-dozen. If I were asked which I consider the best, and which the worst, I am afraid I should have to put that of the Cape peninsula very low on the list, and that of Griqualand West very high—if not the highest on it. But to compare any one of them with those of the Canary Islands, the Azores, and parts of the Riviera in Europe, would to my mind be absurd.

I wish to say a few words only about Cape scenery. While it has some which is squalid and dreary in the extreme, it has much that is most beautiful and even grand. The late Lord Carnarvon on his visit to the Colony said that he had hardly seen anything in Europe more grand and beautiful at the same time than the scenery of the Hex River Mountains. Then we have some famous mountain passes, all more or less grand, such as Bain's Kloof,

Mitchell's Pass, Montague Pass, The Kat Berg, Van
Staaden's Heights, the forests of the Knysna and
Plettenberg's Bay, the lovely slopes of Lower Albany
with its smiling valleys and grassy stretches down to
the Kowie River, which is really an arm of the sea,
navigable by steam-launches as far as about nine or
ten miles from the mouth, the windings of the river,
thickly wooded on both sides, being most picturesque;
British Kaffraria, pronounced by some visitors to have
the most lovely scenery in South Africa; and last, but
certainly not least, is our own Cape peninsula, whose
scenery from simple prettiness to absolute grandeur,
through every intervening variety of beauty, is
scarcely to be surpassed in the world.

CHAPTER XIV.

Our Parliament—Sketches in both Houses.

THIS Colony has produced but one real statesman—
one, however, of such a foremost class as to make him
renowned not only in Europe, but I may say throughout the whole civilized world. No need to name him.
But if none of our public men have not quite attained
to the rank of statesmen, many of them have been
distinguished politicians.

To begin with, I will take the late Mr. Saul Solomon,
who, labouring under terrible physical disadvantages
—for he was but a small dwarf and crippled—made
himself, as a friend of mine termed him, a little
martello tower of strength in the House of Assembly.
He spoke with great fluency, but naturally in a
somewhat shrill voice, and he seemed never to be at
a loss for the word he wanted. He took a large grasp
of most of the subjects which came before the Legislature, and had an eminently practical way of dealing
with them. Like most of us, he had his "fads,"
such as the voluntary principle in religious establish-
ments, which he advocated as if the fate of the
powers depended on it, and his love for the Cape
law of inheritance—happily now repealed; and I
should think it must have been repealed to his own
satisfaction, for he was a bachelor when he fought
for its maintenance, but when somewhat advanced

in years he took unto himself a wife and had a family, and it must have been a satisfaction to him to know that he could distribute his property among them as he pleased.

Then there was Mr. (afterwards Sir John) Molteno, a man of handsome and commanding presence, with a strong, pleasant voice, but, alas! it was not quite pleasant—it always appeared to be forced and unnatural. He, too, had command of plenty of words, and used them with force and effect. His one great political object appeared to be to enforce the introduction of responsible government into the Colony, and for this he fought incessantly. The late Mr. Justice Fitzpatrick once said to me, " I went yesterday to the House of Assembly to hear Molteno speak. I wanted to find out the secret of his success, and I think I have done so. He has no imagination, and is therefore quite unable to illustrate his arguments by tropes and metaphors ; even his arguments are not strong, and he has no tact ; but when he gets hold of an idea he treats it like a big nail, and hammers it until by continued thumping he has driven it into the wood right up to the head." I do not think a better sketch could be made of the honourable gentleman. He was certainly neither a statesman nor an orator, and yet by perseverance and force of character he was enabled to carry his pet scheme and to secure to himself a large and faithful following. He began life a poor man, and, after being farmer, merchant, wool-washer, and land speculator, he realized a very large fortune, to be distributed among a very large family. He was three times married and had children by each wife.

Next I may select the Honourable J. X. Merriman, M.L.A., still in the prime of life and in the full vigour of his mental forces. He is a somewhat stately-looking person with an admirable and flexible voice, and although very fluent his utterance is so distinct that he gives the reporters no trouble. He is an excellent debater—I should say second to none in the House. He is said to be erratic; but this probably means that he is always ready to tackle any subject that presents itself, and treats it from his own point' of view, which occasionally differs from the views of the party for which he is supposed to act. He has great powers of sarcasm, and knows how to use them when the occasion demands it. I think I should be disposed to rank him as almost the most distinguished member of the Cape Parliament. But I know he dislikes flattery, so my eulogy must cease. I have written it, however, the more cordially because I have always suspected the honourable gentleman of disliking me personally—why, I do not know and cannot guess. Perhaps it is another case of "Dr. Fell."

Then there is our present Premier, Sir Gordon Sprigg. Let me start by saying that I know him to be a very hard-working Minister, and I believe him to be a thoroughly conscientious one, and if I point out some of what I consider his defects it must not be supposed I do so to make a feeling of animosity. He is a fluent speaker—we are all fluent speakers in this country—but his voice is somewhat harsh and grating. He nearly always treats the subject very practically, and displays a great amount of firmness and determination. He is accused of a prejudice against our Dutch fellow-Colonists; but I hardly think the accusation is a fair one, though he is no doubt often greatly annoyed at the ignorance and prejudice displayed by many of them, even some who have seats in Parliament, and he gave strong expression to this feeling some time ago in reference to the opposition raised against the Scab Act. He never shirks details, being, in my opinion, a little too fond of them—dealing with matters which might well be left to people with a less exalted position in the service. Thus, some time ago he issued certain regulations requiring every man in the Civil Service from one end of the Colony to the other, and whatever his position might be, to be in his office every morning by 8.30 A.M.—a fairly early hour for breakfast, one would think—thus compelling men who live in the suburbs to rise by lamplight in winter and take breakfast at 7.30 A.M.—a pleasant hour on a cold, rainy, dark morning! Then he fixed the exact time to be allowed to each man for his lunch. Now it would be curious to read *Mr. Punch's* comments on such regulations issued by Mr. Gladstone, Lord Rosebery, or Lord Salisbury. It seems to me that the Premier might have gone a little farther, and specified the exact kinds of viands and liquors to be consumed by each man at his lunch according to his rank in the service. But this perhaps might have got him into hot water, and I believe he prefers putting hot water into himself. He is a stout Free Trader, as he always boasts, though he dallied a little last Session with Protection in regard to the importation of bread stuffs and fresh wheat. He has since declared himself firmly resolved to give no protection to bread stuffs, but I think he is silent about meat, reminding one of the negro sailor at the helm on board his ship. "Hard a port," shouts the captain. "Hard a port it is, sah," answers Sambo; "little 'tarboard same time, sah, eh."

The Hon. Mr. Sauer was, until the other day, the leader of the so-called Opposition; but he has recently been dethroned or has resigned, and his successor, as far as I know, has not yet been chosen. His friends pronounce him the most perfect debater in the House of Assembly, and I shall not dispute their verdict, though I may say that the tones of his voice and his address generally seem to me something approaching the pompous. That he works hard and devours Blue Books as assiduously as any man in Parliament cannot be disputed: thus he is always ready to take part in any discussion, though the subject may often lie somewhat out of the line of his experience or learning. He was one of the three ministers who broke away from Mr. Rhodes' first Administration. I have some doubts if he will ever be asked to join another one.

The Hon. Mr. Innes is also a shining light in our Legislature. Of his ability and general intelligence there can be no doubt. His oratory is not much to my taste, he is a rapid speaker; but his sentences are somewhat jumpy and wanting in "finish," as Mr. Disraeli said of Sir William Harcourt's humour. He is a thorough-going South African patriot—but not a bondsman. His legal acquirements are very great, and his practice as an advocate consequently very large. Altogether, considering that he received his entire education, both scholastic and professional,

H

in this country, he is certainly a remarkable man, and one of whom the Cape Colony is justly proud.

The Hon. Mr. Schreiner, lately Attorney-General, is a man of great learning and great ability. His readiness to deal with any subject—" he is as quick as lightning," said a friend of mine—gives him great force and influence in the House of Assembly. He took high degrees at Cambridge, and whether we regard him as a scholar, a lawyer, or a politician, he is a man in a thousand.

Sir James Sivewright is a man whom I greatly admire. If he is not quite a statesman he makes a nearer approach to the character than any other man, with the exception of our one great statesman. At all events, if he is not a statesman he is a thorough diplomatist, and is the only Cape Colonist who can deal effectively with Oom Paul, whom he is able to smooth down and lead almost as he pleases. The energy and ability he brings to bear on every subject with which he deals stamp him as a born minister. He is equal to the duties of any office in the Cabinet. An admirable, fluent speaker, with a strong Scotch accent, which, when he gets excited, becomes powerful enough to transport you veritably to the Land o' Cakes; he has certainly no match in the present Cabinet.

After these few selections from the House of Assembly it might be supposed that I should have something to say about the Legislative Council. But with the exception of the President, there is hardly a member of it who has made much stir, or indeed attempted to make one in politics. But there are one or two sturdy model legislators in it. Take, for instance, the Hon. W. Ross, a straightforward, honest, and plain-spoken man, never hesitating to call a spade by its real name, and quite careless as to what posing critics may say of him. He speaks as earnestly as he thinks.

Then there is the Hon. Mr. Faure, a Cabinet Minister, not only a conscientious man devoted to his duties, but one of finished urbanity and courteous manner; yet he knows how to administer a snub when he pleases, which comes all the more forcibly from so unpretentious a man.

Perhaps it may be thought that I ought here to give some account of my own political career, for I have at different times represented four separate divisions of the Colony in our Parliament, namely, those of the Cape, Albert, King Williams Town, and Colesberg. I did my duty to the best of my ability in the House of Assembly, taking part in many debates and making a number of speeches, some of which were extravagantly praised, and others— perhaps more justly — roundly abused. Neither favourable nor hostile criticism moved me much; but I must frankly confess I was never able to throw myself heart and soul into Cape politics; I could never attach myself to any particular party, probably being unable to understand the principles which guided it, and thus I was never a strong partisan.

> "In moderation placing all my glory,
> While Tories called me Whig, and Whigs a Tory."

Let no one suppose that in writing thus I mean to depreciate the pursuit of politics either in the mother country or here, or that I for a moment agree with that very dogmatic old gentleman, Dr. Samuel Johnson, who declared politics to be the last refuge of a scoundrel.   On the contrary, I believe that many of the legislators in this country and at home are actuated by the highest motives, desirous of promoting the welfare and prosperity of the land they live in.   If I have been unable to follow or imitate them I can only cry *mea culpa, mea culpa*.

CHAPTER XV.

Some Judicial Experiences of my Own and some of other Judges.

THE life of the Cape judge is a peculiar one when compared with a judge in England. Occasionally, but not very often, he has very little to do ; but at other times he is so overwhelmed with work that it is difficult for him to get through it. This is especially the case with the Criminal Sessions and with Circuits generally. The interpretation takes up a great deal of time in Court : thus, supposing a prisoner to be a Hottentot, who understands no language but Cape Dutch, a Kafir witness is called who understands scarcely a word of any tongue but his own, then the interpreter understands Kafir and Dutch, but not English ; he has to interpret from Kafir into Dutch, while another interpreter has to interpret from Dutch to English, so that the judge may make his notes of what is said. All this is very wearisome, especially as there is no authorised shorthand writer to save the judge's time by taking down the evidence, and afterwards turning it into the usual long hand. It would be a great saving of time, labour, and expense—for the longer a Circuit Court lasts the greater expense to the country—if a Government shorthand writer were appointed to each Circuit Court.

Then the interpretation is often very unsatisfactory,

if not so much in taking the evidence as in giving the judge's summing-up to the jury. Many of them break down over this test, and Mr. Justice Cloete once performed the extraordinary feat of first addressing a jury—and it was a long address—in English, and afterwards recommencing translating all that he had said in Dutch. I was told by one who heard it, and was better able to judge of it than myself, that the translation was simply perfect. The late Mr. Serrurier, in the Supreme Court, when there were Dutchmen on the jury, used to make them sit at one end of the jury box next to which he stood and rattle them off the judge's address as he went on, without the slightest interruption. But such men are not to be met with in Circuit towns. The present interpreter of the Supreme Court is a most accomplished gentleman, being the master of at least three or four languages, and he is quite capable of doing as his predecessors did ; but then his services are available on the Western Circuit only, the other two Circuits having to depend on such interpreters as may from such and such a time turn up. I took the Northern Circuit three times and never had the same interpreter on each.

The status of a judge is very highly appreciated in this country, and I doubt whether the occupants of the Bench are treated with greater respect anywhere else than they meet with on all sides in this country. This may be partly owing to the fact that by the Charter of Justice their rank is fixed above that of all other Colonists after the Governor and the General commanding the forces. But I think there are other causes at work. Their half-yearly visit to every town in which the Circuit Court is held is eagerly looked forward to by the inhabitants of the places, and on their arrival there are received with as much reverence as a Royal prince would be at home. It is customary for the Circuit Judge to give a dinner-party in each Circuit town, to which are invited the magistrate, the sheriff, the district surgeon, clergymen of the English and Dutch Churches, some other officials, and as many members of the Bar as the table will accommodate.

These dinners are greatly enjoyed, bringing the inhabitants of remote places in contact with those freshly from the capital. Naturally the success of the entertainments depends considerably on the judge himself and his possession of *bonhomie*. I have been present at some judges' dinners which seemed to cast a wet blanket over everybody present, owing to the want of geniality on the part of the host, and I have known others of the liveliest description, where the jests circulated as freely as the dishes and the wine. The clergymen of both churches, to do them justice, often contribute greatly to the success of the feast, being men of intelligence and learning. At a dinner given by myself where the fun was going on well, a barrister at the bottom of the table cried out to me—

"Judge, they are beginning to talk religion up here."

"Good gracious!" I exclaimed, "are we already so drunk as that?"

At which there was a laugh; but, seriously, I have often observed the tendency of people, who have had more wine than they are accustomed, to fall into theological discussions. I may say, however, that I have never known anything like excess to prevail at the Circuit dinners.

When a judge travels in this country a whole carriage of five compartments is assigned to him, for the conveyance of himself, his registrar, his servants, and his baggage, and no one is allowed to enter the sacred precincts of this carriage except the judicial party and such friends as the judge may choose to invite. When he travels by road away from the line of railway he is provided with a large travelling spring waggon drawn by eight horses, and which carries his servants, his luggage, and his travelling stock of provisions, wines, &c. It is customary on his approaching a Circuit town for him to be met by a party of Mounted Volunteers or Cape Mounted Police, to escort him into town, making quite an imposing cavalcade. I forgot to mention that for the judge's own use is provided either a Cape cart or, better still, an American spider carriage drawn by four horses. Like other travellers he has of course to outspan for breakfast and luncheon, and to enjoy those meals in the open air.

On one occasion a judge whose equipages were outspanned, and who was very fond of a little pedestrianism, set off to walk by himself towards the town to which he was bound, telling his people to follow him when they were ready. On his road he was met by a file of Cape Mounted Police with a sergeant at their head, who cried out to him—

" I say, old fellow, where is the judge ? "

" Oh, you'll find his waggons at the outspan place."

" All right, we'll have a drink, old chap," producing a flask from his pocket.

" No, thank you," said the judge.

" Oh, come, old chap, don't say no."

" But I really must refuse," said the judge.

" Well, then you are a jolly old muff, that's all."

When the sergeant reached the outspan place the equipages were just about ready to start.

" Where's the judge ? " asked the sergeant of the butler.

" Why, you must have met him on foot," answered the butler.

" No, we didn't," replied the sergeant.

" Why there is only one road, and he went off on that one."

The sergeant looked a little grave and asked how the judge was dressed. The butler gave an accurate but perhaps not a very flattering description of his master's travelling costume.

" Hulloa ! " cries the sergeant, " was that the judge ? By jove, and I called him a jolly old muff ! What shall I do now ? "

" Oh, don't trouble yourself," said the butler ; " the judge is very good-natured, and he won't take any notice of your mistake."

Nor did he, for when the party overtook him on the road the sergeant drew up his men on salute point and the judge returned the salute before entering his carriage without giving any other recognition of the sergeant or his men.

Another curious incident occurred with regard to the same judge. He was in a Circuit town and was returning home to his lodgings from a very early morning walk, when he went into a chemist's shop and asked for a bottle of soda water.

"All right, old gentleman," said the smart youth behind the counter; "I see what it is—hot coppers, eh?"

"It's nothing of the kind, I'm Mr. Justice ——"

"Oh, lor!" cries the assistant. "I beg pardon, my Lord; I didn't know your Lordship. I beg ——"

"Oh, never mind," said the judge, "there's no harm done," and, paying for his soda water, walked away.

Now this judge was not only a very learned one but as amiable and good-tempered a man as could be found. It seemed impossible that he could ever have known what anger was. But he was certainly not of commanding aspect, and this probably accounts for the two mistakes I have chronicled.

I may here relate two curious incidents in my own judicial career. I was one day going down to my chambers, and had very nearly reached them, when I was accosted by an Irishwoman.

"Plaise, me Lard, may I spake to you?"

"Certainly, what is it?"

"Ye see, me Lard, my husband has been behaving very badly to me, and yesterday he took to baiting me, and I want you to give me a divorce from him."

"Yes, but when—where?"

"At wunst, me Lard."

"What here, where we are?"

"Af it plaise ye, me Lard, yes."

I told her that I had no power to do that and she must bring an action against her husband and have it properly tried in Court. I asked her if she knew any respectable attorney in town, but she did not, so I told her to go and see my clerk and he would advise her where to go to. She was grateful but looked a little disappointed at the law's delays, evidently thinking it rather hard that she couldn't get a divorce in the street without her husband knowing anything about it.

The other incident occurred while travelling on Circuit. When we came to Carlisle Bridge, in the division of Albany, where there is a toll-bar, the toll-keeper came up to my carriage—he was an Irishman—and said—

"I don't think I can ask ye Lardship for any toll."

"Why not?" I asked.

"Well, ye see, me Lard, ye're riding in one of the Queen's carriages"—it had the Royal arms on the panel—"and the Queen pays no tolls."

I told him that that was perfectly true in England, but the judges on Circuit had always paid tolls, and that while the half-crown might be of some service to him, I did not think the Cape Government would miss it. He took the toll but looked rather disturbed in his conscience at doing so. I wonder what Mr. Weller senior would have said of such a pikeman.

This recalls to me a story which I fear may be a "chestnut," but I shall risk repeating it.

Sir Walter Scott and an Irish gentleman were having a little friendly controversy concerning the loyalty of their respective countrymen. The discussion went on well enough, and neither party seemed to give it up, when the Irishman said suddenly—

"Now look at this as a specimen of Irish loyalty.

When the King—George IV.—was over in Ireland lately he passed with his retinue through a certain turnpike gate, nobody, of course, thinking of stopping him, the toll-keeper himself waving his cap over his head and shouting, Hurrah for the King ; but the worthy Pat on the other side of the road noticed this, and as soon as the cavalcade had passed he went up to the toll-man and said—

" ' What for didn't ye git ye toll ? '

" ' Sure,' said the man, ' I couldn't ask the King to pay me.'

" ' And de ye think,' says Pat, ' that I'd let his Majesty be beholden to the likes of ye for his toll. No ; there's your money,' " pulling some silver from his pocket.

Sir Walter Scott, laughing, said—

" Well, I give it up now.   I confess I don't believe any countryman of my own would ever think of offering to pay the King's toll for him."

CHAPTER XVI.

My Success at the Bar—The Rules which guided me.

Some strange scenes have occurred in my practice at the Cape Bar, perhaps more in criminal than in civil cases. I had once to defend a prisoner charged with uttering base coin; he pleaded not guilty, and a jury having been called, the Registrar pointed to them and put the usual question to the prisoner—

"Do you object to being tried by any of these gentlemen?"

"I do," he answered.

"Which of them?"

"I object to the whole lot of them."

I suggested, "Perhaps you object to being tried at all?"

"I do, sar."

But as we couldn't accommodate him in that respect the case had to go on. The coins, which were pretended half-crowns, were produced, evidently made of pewter and a shockingly bad imitation of any coin in the world. I suggested that the attempt to pass must have been a practical joke, as it was impossible that anybody could be deceived by such things. But it appeared that the prisoner and another man used to go late in the evening to some shop hardly lighted at all by a dip candle, and, selecting some article worth about a penny, would hand over one of these imitations and get the change for it, and in this manner several tradesmen were victimised, so the prisoner was very properly convicted.

My success in the defence of criminal cases was great, and occasionally surprised myself; but I had laid down three rules for my own guidance from which I never departed.

The first was, never to import myself into the case —that is to say, never to press my own personal opinions on it to the jury. It always appeared to me to be a degradation to the profession for a barrister to use such sentences as "I firmly believe so and so," though I am aware this has been done by a few men in England distinguished for their advocacy in criminal cases.

The second was, never to bully a witness in cross-examination, if it was possible to avoid it. I always preferred the *suaviter in modo*, endeavouring to get on friendly terms with the witness, and apparently accepting the truth of what he said until I had led him on to the pit-fall I had laid for him, and into which he ignominiously flopped. I have bullied a witness when I knew him to be a shameless scoundrel. On one occasion a witness whom I was pressing very hard fainted twice, or pretended to faint, during the cross-examination, and had to be carried out of Court. When he presented himself in the box a third time I declined to ask him a single further question, telling the judge that the answers I had already elicited and the witness' demeanour in the box were quite sufficient for the support of my case.

The late Baron Huddlestone prided himself greatly on his cross-examining powers, but he one day met his match in a witness on Circuit. This was a horse-dealer in Cheltenham, named Jacobs. Mr. Huddlestone knew all about him, and often expressed his wish to get that fellow into the box, when he thought he would turn him inside out. The opportunity at last occurred, and in a case which Mr. Huddlestone was defending—a horse-dealing case—Jacobs was called by the plaintiff as a witness. When the time for cross-examination occurred, Mr. Huddlestone stood up and, looking hard at the witness, said—

" Now then, Jacobs."

" Now then, Huddlestone," says the witness.

Mr. Huddlestone was terribly taken back by surprise. The idea of addressing *him*, the great shining light on his Circuit, and married to the daughter of a Duke, in such an insolent manner was too much for him. He looked up at the judge and the judge turning to the witness said—

" You must treat the learned counsel with proper respect."

Begging your Lordship's pardon," said the witness, " look here, the counsel addresses me in the most familiar terms, and calls me Jacobs, as if I had no right to a handle to my name; I'm sure your Lordship would never have treated me in that style."

Mr. Huddlestone was here about to interfere when Jacobs, waving his hand to him, said—

" Wait a minute, Mr. Huddlestone, I'm talking to a *gentleman* now; when I have done with him I shall be ready for *you*."

The examination then went on.

" Well, then, *Mr.* Jacobs," said Huddlestone.

" Well, then, *Mr.* Huddlestone," said Jacobs.

But the witness was terribly astute and foiled Mr. Huddlestone at every point, so that he threw himself into his seat saying—

"I can do nothing with this witness, my Lord."

"No," said Jacobs, *sotto voce*, but loud enough to be heard by the Court, "I never thought you would."

The third principle to which I always adhered was to watch carefully the countenances of the jurymen whom I was addressing, so as to see whether they were agreeing or disagreeing with me. Occasionally I would see five or six apparently approving of what I said, and the rest three or four looking quite unconvinced; for the benefit of these last I would recapitulate some of my arguments with fresh illustrations, till I could see by their looks that they were coming round to my views. Of course this could not always be done, and I could see two or three determined not to be convinced; then there was nothing for it but to make up one's mind to an adverse verdict.

Again, the race of the jurymen influenced me. I should not think of addressing a Boer jury in the same style as an English one. With a mixed jury your arguments had also to be mixed. I made a few allowances for the peculiar views which I knew would be taken by the men of different race.

At Queenstown once I had to defend an Englishman charged with flogging his Kafir servant most unmercifully. The jury were all Englishmen born, and I knew my men, therefore one great point I made was this—

"Do you Englishmen think which is more likely —that a Kafir—you know the people pretty well—

—should come here and lie, or that an Englishman, your own countryman, should commit the atrocities imputed to him?"

This is, of course, a mere outline of what I used; but I could see by the faces of the jury that I had hit the right nail on the head. Notwithstanding a severe summing up by the judge against the prisoner, he was acquitted triumphantly without the jury having even left the box to consult.

The next day, meeting the judge, he said—

"That was a very good idea of yours, Cole; but, after all, which lied? Was it the Kafir?"

"Well," I replied, "the jury seemed to think so; and, you see, we can't go behind the verdict of the jury. He laughed and said—

"Of course not; and you knew how to deal with a jury of John Bulls."

One of the most important cases I was ever engaged in was that of a rich Dutch farmer in the Beaufort West district, who was charged with the wilful murder of his Kafir servant boy, whom I had to defend. The case excited the utmost interest, as the man was not only wealthy himself, but had a large number of rich and influential relatives. The case lasted from nine o'clock in the morning till past ten o'clock at night, with about two half-hour intervals for refreshment. Thus I may say we actually worked for full twelve hours, when a verdict of "Not guilty" was returned by the jury, and I impute this greatly to the ignorance of the judge, the jury, and myself on one point. The evidence showed that the accused had violently and brutally thrashed the deceased boy with a sjambok, and it was said that death was the

I

result of the beating. At a *post-mortem* examination it was found that there was a fig entirely undigested in the stomach of the lad. I asked the district surgeon how long a fig took to digest? and his answer was "fifteen to twenty minutes"; while it was proved that the death had not occurred till at least an hour and a half after the beating. I then put it to the jury that the boy after the beating must have been well enough to go to the orchard, which was a little distance from the house, and get this fig found undigested. The judge, in summing up to the jury, strongly impressed on them this argument of mine, which he considered most important, the result being, as I have said, an acquittal of the prisoner. It will be seen by what I have said, of which I have given the merest sketch of the arguments on the occasion, I never placed reliance on one shot only. The cheers of the audience on hearing the verdict were tremendous, and I narrowly escaped being carried out of Court on the shoulders of enthusiastic Boers.

Next morning in the street I fell in with the district surgeon himself, who said—

"You did that very well, Mr. Cole; but I suppose you know the explanation about the fig?"

"I give you my word of honour I do not, if you mean there is some explanation which disposes of my argument, for I never intentionally mislead a jury."

"Well, then, I'll tell you," he said. "The frightful beating the boy received would completely suspend all powers of digestion, and thus the fig which was found in the boy was probably one that he had just stolen, and for which he received the beating."

I told him I was shocked, as I was sure the judge would be, that the ignorance of both of us should have so influenced the jury.

"But," I added, "why did you not give us this information in Court?"

"Well, I never was asked any question to which that would have been an answer," he said.

Which was true; but it struck me that he might easily have given the information at the time when I asked him the question as to how long the fig took to digest? But then the prisoner had, as I said before, many rich and influential friends and relatives in and about Beaufort West, and a district surgeon must live chiefly on the fees of his patients, for the Government pay is too small for the purpose.

I have one incident to relate of entirely different character to the last. Jan, a Hottentot prisoner, was charged at the Worcester Circuit Court with a malicious and violent assault on somebody. The indictment was read by the Registrar, and then translated into Dutch, being the prisoner's own language. When he had heard it to the end, Jan said—

"No, baas, I don't know anything about that; I'm the boy that stole Mr. Jones's pony."

There was of course a good deal of laughter—they had brought up the wrong Jan, so he was temporarily removed from the dock, and the other Jan took his place. But the best of it was that, when the first Jan was again put in the dock, and properly indicted for stealing Mr. Jones's pony, he boldly pleaded "Not guilty." And he managed to get off; my argument in his favour being that, when he said "I am the boy that stole Mr. Jones's pony," he only meant "I am the boy *charged* with stealing Mr. Jones's pony."

One of the strangest successes I ever had—when, indeed, I was even sorry to succeed—was brought about by what I may call an accident. It was at a Middelburg Circuit Court. The day before the sitting of the Court I received a note from the judge —Watermeyer—saying that there were two bushmen in gaol charged with murder, and the case appeared to him a most atrocious one. He didn't suppose that anything could be done with the prisoners, but he did not like to try a man for his life without giving him the advantage of a counsel's assistance ; would I, therefore, kindly take the case? Of course I assented ; but, after reading the preliminary examinations, I saw before me nothing but a most hopeless task. I went down to the gaol and saw the men, who were two hideous little bushmen. I asked the interpreter to tell them that they must make up their minds to be hanged. They had a look of stoical indifference, as these people always have in matters of life and death. Then I asked them to give me the indictments with which they had been served, and they handed them to me. Turning them over I made a discovery, which, however, I did not choose to communicate to the prisoners. Next day the case was called on, and the men placed in the dock. The Registrar stood up to read the indictment, but I stopped him, and said—

"My Lord, these men have never been served with a notice of trial."

"Oh, yes, they have," cried Mr. Barry, who was the prosecuting counsel. "I'll call the sheriff to prove the service."

" Oh, yes," I said, " that's all right, and I hold the two copies of the indictment with which they were served in my hand. The law requires that notice of trial on the back of an indictment shall be signed either by the Attorney-general or his clerk, or the clerk to the magistrate of the town in which the Circuit Court is to be held. The notices in this case have never been served at all "—holding them up.

" Oh, well," said Mr. Barry, " that can be remedied at once; I'll get the clerk to sign the notices now."

I laughed, and said—

" No, that won't do at all. I'll leave the matter to his Lordship."

" Mr. Barry," said the judge, " it is quite clear that the law is peremptory, and that notices of trial must be signed by either of the three officers mentioned by Mr. Cole before they are served; therefore I must postpone this case to the next Circuit Court here."

" Oh, no," I said, " begging your Lordship's pardon, the law requires that every prisoner committed for trial at any Circuit Court, shall be brought to trial before the next sitting of that Court before his committal. The trial may be postponed on cause shown to the next Circuit Court, but at that second Circuit Court, if he is not brought to trial, he is entitled to his release, and cannot be re-arrested on the same charge. This is the second sitting of the Court in regard to these prisoners, and they have not been brought to trial."

Mr. Barry continued that they had been brought to trial, as they were then in the dock; but, as I pointed out, the judge had already ruled they were not *legally* brought to trial, and therefore I applied for their discharge.

The judge looked very grave indeed, and said—

"Mr. Cole, I will not say whether I agree with you or not, but this is really too serious a matter for me to decide sitting here by myself, so I must reserve the point to be argued in the Supreme Court, the prisoners to remain in custody until the question has been decided."

Of course I made no objections, and shortly afterwards the case was heard before the full Bench in Cape Town, then consisting of four judges, when it was unanimously decided that my contention was right, and an order was made for the prisoners to be released. I very much doubt if they ever knew why they were released.

I was chaffed a little by some of my friends, who told me I ought to be ashamed of letting two blood-thirsty murderers loose upon society. My reply was, "that as far as this Colony was concerned, they might be sure that the prisoners would clear out of it as quickly as possible, and give it a very wide berth in the future, besides which," I added, "I had saved the Colony some two or three hundred pounds, as it would have cost quite that to hang the little brutes."

CHAPTER XVII.

Cape Literature, principally Newspaper and Periodical—My own connection with it.

WHEN the *cacœthes scribendi* has once seized a man it seldom leaves him; it was therefore very unlikely that it should desert me, who had for some time at home depended chiefly on my pen for a livelihood. My contributions, however, to the literature of the Colony were chiefly fugitive pieces, and I suppose not of much importance. Indeed, a writer in the *Cape Times* who lately enumerated the different South African writers, omitted my name altogether, probably considering myself and my productions beneath his notice.

I was for some few years an editor of the *Cape Monthly Magazine,** and almost regularly contributed an article to each number. I also, from time to time, wrote leading articles for different newspapers. The only collective work I ever published in the Cape was the " Three Idylls of a Prince," written on the occasion of the Duke of Edinburgh's (the Prince Alfred's) first visit to the Cape. Sir George Grey took a great fancy to my verses, and begged me to reprint them, as they had only appeared in a newspaper, and he also asked me to have a few handsomely bound presentation copies made, as he wished to send some home to certain members of the Royal family. This was done, and I had the gratification some months

* Published by J. C. Juta & Co.

later of being assured by Sir George that Her Majesty and the Princess Royal had been heartily amused by reading my nonsense verses.   On the occasion of the Duke of Edinburgh's second visit to the Cape, I wrote " The People's Ball," meaning the ball given to him by the people of Cape Town, and " The Elephant Hunt," commemorating the killing of an elephant in the Knysna forest by the Prince and some of his friends. Mr. Justice Fitzpatrick once read this last at a public entertainment in Grahamstown, and created great amusement by the extraordinary manner in which he pronounced the single Dutch line in it. To the *Cape Monthly Magazine* I also contributed " The Flight of the Amakosa," *à propos* of the escape of some Kafir prisoners from the gaol of the Amsterdam Battery ; and the " Shank End Shindy," commemorative of a meeting held in Cape Town to condemn the proceeding of the Parliament, then sitting for the first and last time in Grahamstown. All these were *à la* Ingoldsby.   There may be some others which escape my memory at the moment.

I had almost forgotten, by the way, my " Lay of the Post Cart," which was taken over, I think, by almost every newspaper in the Colony, and has been quoted quite recently in a work written in or on South Africa.

When I came to the Colony in 1856 there were three newspapers published in Cape Town, and an advertising sheet which was distributed *gratis*, and depended for profit only on the advertisements it contained.   The three newspapers were the *Commercial Advertiser*, *The Mail*, and the *Zuid Afrikaan*, which was published one-half in English and the other half in Dutch ; the former two were in English only. None of these were published more than three times a week—a daily paper being then unknown in the Colony. The *Commercial Advertiser* was edited by the late Mr. John Fairbairn, the father of the present Clerk of the Legislative Council. Its leading articles were admirable, for Mr. Fairbairn was a scholar, and a man of extensive information and great literary ability. It is said that he was once offered a permanent position on the staff of the. London *Times*, but, fortunately for the Colony, he declined the offer, and remained to delight and enlighten the people of Cape Town. He had a seat in the House of Assembly in the first Cape Parliament, and was put forward as a candidate for the Speakership; but the House wanted a lawyer in the chair, and, consequently, chose Mr. C. J. (afterwards Sir Christoffel) Brand. It was well that the matter was so settled, for the House got a fairly good Speaker in Mr. Brand, though he was by no means. the genius his friends declared him to be, and was certainly not as able a Speaker as his successor, Sir David Tennant. On the other hand, Mr. Fairbairn was left free to use his pen in the cause of freedom and progress, which he never failed to advocate. Indeed, it may be said that it is to him the Colony.. was indebted for a free and independent press. He died when I had been only a few years in the Colony, and I was never on very intimate terms with him, but I knew him well enough to admire and respect him, and to value his scholarship. I was pleased to find that his favourite Latin poet, like my own, was Horace, of whom he once said, " he is not only a .

complete man of the world, but such a gentleman," which was a very good description of the asthmatic little poet.

The *Commercial Advertiser* subsequently passed into other hands, but it ceased to have the influence which it possessed when under the guidance of Mr. Fairbairn.

The Mail, which had been edited by Mr. Charles Cowen—still alive, I believe, and I hope as vigorous and energetic as ever—subsequently passed into other hands, and ceased to exist, or rather became amalgamated with another paper, which took the name of the *South African Advertiser and Mail,* and was for some time edited by Mr. John Noble, the talented Clerk of the House of Assembly.

The *Zuid Afrikaan* is still extant, and as lively as ever.

In January, 1857, the first daily paper published in the Colony appeared under the title of the *Cape Argus,* and I contributed to its first number. Messrs. B. H. Darnell and R. W. Murray, senior, were its proprietors, Mr. Darnell principally writing the leading articles, and Mr. Murray performing the difficult task of collecting news and generally getting up the paper. In those days Cape Town was but a small place, and one can hardly imagine how a paper could be filled with readable matter when there were no telegraphs, inland posts only running three times a week or less, and the monthly mail steamers from England occupying thirty to thirty-five days on each voyage. But Mr. Murray was always a man of ready resources, and made his paper a great improvement on any that had preceded it. As a "leader" writer Mr. Darnell has had only one worthy successor, for his pen was graphic, caustic, and full of energy and determination ; his language being always apt and well chosen. He was perhaps the most outspoken man I have ever met with, apparently totally indifferent to praise or censure. He, too, had a seat in the House of Assembly ; he was a slow and somewhat laboured speaker, and may almost be said to have a tendency to hesitation over his words, but he said keen and stinging things, as for example—

"David said in his haste that 'all men are liars;' if he had lived in this Colony he would have said it at his leisure."

"Of course, the honourable member excepts himself," said somebody.

"No, I don't," was the reply. "I have lived here long enough to be acclimatised."

After a time the partnership between Messrs. Darnell and Murray was dissolved, Mr. Darnell taking up farming at the Knysna, and Mr. Murray going to Grahamstown, where he established a new paper called the *Eastern Star*. Meanwhile the *Cape Argus* had passed into the hands of Mr. Saul Solomon, when its political character became entirely changed, and the principal editor was the late Professor Roderic Noble, and subsequently Mr. T. E. Fuller. It remained the property of Mr. Solomon's firm until taken over by Mr. F. J. Dormer, who eventually transferred it to the "Argus Printing Company," of which he was the founder and managing director. It is now edited by a Mr. Powell, whose leading articles I seldom omit to read, because they are not only well written, but honest and

straightforward, leaving no doubt on the reader's
mind of what the writer means.

The *Cape Times* is the latest addition to the daily
press of Cape Town, although it is already several
years old. It has a circulation vastly exceeding any
that could have been dreamt of in my early days
in the Colony. This, I think, may be attributed
especially to two causes—first, to the untiring energy
of Mr. Murray, junior, in keeping up the supply of
news; and secondly and mainly, to the admirable
leading articles written by Mr. F. Y. St. Leger.
He was the worthy successor to Mr. Darnell that I
spoke of, and perhaps even more skilful and polished
in his writings than his predecessor. Though still
continuing the proprietor of the *Cape Times*, Mr.
St. Leger has recently resigned the editorship,
taking no active part in the management. *Plorant*
lectores.

Cape Town has possessed and still possesses a
few other periodicals, but they are mostly of a
sectarian kind, and fitted for those who like to discuss sacred subjects in newspapers. But as I have
no sympathy with them, I make a point of never
reading their papers.

It would, of course, be impossible for me to give
an outline sketch of the many newspapers published
throughout the Colony, some of them in the larger
towns being of a high standard, and directed by
men of learning and talent; only a very few of
them are published daily. The Western province
of the Colony, however, is still terribly deficient in
this branch of literature, for Dutch farmers, who
compose the majority of its population, care little

for news not immediately and personally affecting
them, and nothing at all for literature in general.

We have no " Cape Magazine," nor does anything
of the kind worthy of mention exist in the Colony,
with the exception of a Roman Catholic Magazine,
which can never fail to be interesting as long as it
is under the guidance of the Rev. Dr. Kolbe, and
can boast of such a contributor as the Rev. Dr.
McCarthy. There is also a Law Journal, very wel-
come to the legal profession, and under the able
editorship of Mr. C. H. van Zyl—a lawyer whose
legal learning can scarcely be surpassed by any
barrister in the country.

P.S.—In the above enumeration of Cape daily
papers I accidentally omitted the name of the
Standard, which was started many years ago under
the auspices of Mr. T. B. Bayley, and edited by Mr.
William Foster. Its principal object was to make
a determined opposition against the introduction of
Responsible Government. It had a very fair success
for some years, but after the death of Mr. Bayley
the funds, I fancy, fell low, and the public support
not being sufficient for its maintenance, it suddenly
collapsed, to the great grief of some gentlemen who
had invested capital in it. Besides which, when
Responsible Government had been actually introduced, it had scarcely a *raison d'être*. Perhaps I
may mention a curious little incident connecting me
with the paper. A case of great importance had
been decided in the Supreme Court, and on the day
when the report of it appeared, Mr. Foster called
upon me at my chambers, and asked me whether I
would write a leader on the subject for his paper,

as he knew no man so well able to deal with it. I consented to do so, and, just as he was leaving my room, Mr. Fuller entered it. He also came to ask me to write a leader on the same subject for his paper. Not wishing him to suspect my connection with the other paper, I after a little hesitation consented. I therefore set to work and wrote two leading articles, one for each of the two papers, both coming to the same conclusion on the matter, but treating it from entirely different points of view. Next morning the two rival journals appeared, each with mine as its principal leader, and in the course of the day each of the editors called upon me, thanking me for what I had done, and each of them declaring that he thought the article in his paper very superior to that of the other. If I did not laugh outright it showed my command over my risible faculties.

CHAPTER XVIII.

The Present Condition of the Cape Bench and Bar, with Sketches from each.

IN discussing the present state of the Cape Bench, I naturally commence with the Chief Justice Sir Henry de Villiers, who has just been created Privy Councillor. He is really a very remarkable man, for he is not only a profound lawyer and able politician, but he possesses great taste in literature and art. He has, of course, a perfect command of the English, Dutch, and Latin languages, and this knowledge adds greatly to his efficiency as judge. His judgments are always learned, without being in any degree pedantic, and are couched in such apt language as to make them perfectly comprehensible to professional men and lay men alike. I do not think he has ever given offence to any one, for his tact and courtesy are perfect. That he is the ablest Chief Justice the Colony has ever seen I firmly believe ; at all events, his two immediate predecessors could not compare with him. As President of the Legislative Council he maintains the dignity of his position without any ostentation, and his influence over its members is so great that almost a mere hint of his is sometimes sufficient to decide the fate of a measure. He started in life without any advantages of fortune ; but his quiet energy and determination were sufficient to overcome any obstacles. He was

called to the Bar of the Inner Temple, and coming
out here to practise, made his mark from the com-
mencement, and he was only thirty-two years of age
when he became Chief Justice of the Colony, having
previously been Attorney-General. I take to myself
some credit for having prophesied his success from
the very first, and when he was raised to his present
position, I received a letter from Ireland, from my
old friend Mr. William Porter, in which he said:
" I often think how you foretold De Villiers' success,
and possibly I was not quite so sanguine as yourself,
but even you, I think, could hardly have expected
him to attain to his present position at so early an
age." Of course not, because I could not have
foreseen the current of events which led to his being
first Attorney-General and then Chief Justice. Every
one will approve of the bestowal of the last new
honour upon him.

By his side as first Puisne Judge sits Mr. Justice
Buchanan, a clear-headed, well-read lawyer—his
Reports would alone prove that—and one of the
most amiable of men. On his elevation to the Bench
I wrote to a friend : " In some of the schools in this
Colony a prize is given to the best-liked boy ; if a
prize were to be given to the best-liked barrister of
the Supreme Court, it would be awarded by acclama-
tion to Buchanan."

The other Puisne Judge sitting in the Supreme
Court is Mr. Justice Maasdorp, who has made his
way to his present position by ability and industry,
and he, too, is a very much-liked man.

The Judge President of the Court of the Eastern
Districts is Sir Jacob Barry—one of the most hard-

working, conscientious judges I have ever known. He is also a man of great personal courage, which is no mean gift to a South African judge. I have seen him when at the Bar drive a pair of horses through the foaming drift of a river, he sitting up to his waist in water, and when a very slight swerving of the horses might have carried him, them, and the vehicle he was driving to almost certain destruction. He was the only coachman, professional or otherwise, who dared to face that drift on that occasion. He was for some time Recorder of Griqualand West when that territory was separate from the Cape of Good Hope, and had its own High Court and its one judge. While occupying that position he was suddenly called upon to act as Administrator of the Government of that Province. Something very like an armed rebellion broke out in Kimberley, but he was equal to the occasion, and, by dint of pluck, quickness, and determination, he succeeded in quelling it without bloodshed, and in an incredibly short time. For this and other services he received his knighthood, and no honour was ever better deserved.

On his right hand in Court sits Mr. Justice Jones, a most indefatigable judge and a graduate of Cambridge, being, I think, the first Cape Colonist upon whom the University bestowed the degree of LL.M., which I believe he has since exchanged for the higher one of LL.D. At all events he ought to have had it.

On the left of the Judge President sits Mr. Justice Solomon, a man whose judgments are admired for their clearness and logic, and who, in the gravity of his appearance, is every inch a judge. Indeed, though

K

comparatively a young man, he looks—and is—as wise as if he was seventy.

The High Court of Griqualand is presided over by Mr. Justice Laurence. It would be really difficult to speak in too high terms of this gentleman's ability. At Cambridge he took almost every degree—especially in law—that the University could confer on him, including the Chancellor's Gold Medal. He is equally at home in classics and mathematics, and has acted as examiner in each at the Cape University. His judgments are profound and elaborate—perhaps a little too elaborate sometimes—and are greatly respected by the profession for the learning and research they display. He is a man of literary tastes, too, and if Kimberley does not owe to him its public library it is at least indebted to him for the condition in which it at present exists, second in the Colony only, I think, to that of Cape Town. His annual addresses, as chairman of the committee, are always anticipated with pleasure, and he exercises great discrimination and taste in the selection of books of every description as far as the funds at his command will permit him. He has one great defect—he is an inveterate bachelor.

The judge on his right hand is Mr. Justice Hopley, formerly a pupil of my own, and I am proud to have had anything to do with the training of so acute and able a lawyer. He is the handsomest man on the Bench—I hope the other judges will not be offended at this—but as, with one exception, they are all married, it cannot injure their prospects.

On the left of the Judge President sits Mr. Justice Lange, only recently raised to the Bench. He for

some time held the office of Prosecutor in the Special
I. D. B. Court, and his learning and experience will
be of great value to the Bench. He is the prince
of good fellows, and cannot have an enemy in the
world.

I may remark as a curious fact that neither of the
three judges sitting in the Supreme Court has taken
a University degree, while each of the other six of
the Eastern Districts and Griqualand benches is a
graduate of the University of Cambridge.

In attempting a sketch of the Bar as it now exists,
I shall be obliged to select only a few of its members
as examples. To begin with, there is the Attorney-
General, Sir Thomas Upington. He occupied a seat
on the Bench of the Supreme Court for some two or
more years, but he suddenly resigned that position
in order to become, for the third or fourth time,
Attorney-General of the Colony. I fancy that the
somewhat placid monotony of judicial life jarred
upon him, for, as Byron says, " quiet to quick bosoms
is a hell," and if ever a man possessed a quick
bosom, it is my friend Sir Thomas Upington. But
be the cause what it may, he has returned to the
arena of politics and law, ready to take his part in
the contests of both. As a lawyer, his reputation is
of the highest; as an advocate, his quickness of
apprehension, command of language, and skill in
dealing with witnesses, make him, I think, unrivalled
here. He is ready for anything, from prosecuting
criminals and arguing points of law to fighting rebels,
as he did on the northern border a few years ago,
exposing himself to perils by flood and field which
might have taxed the strongest constitution, while

he is somewhat fragile. But, after all, I think it is pluck, rather than bodily strength, that pulls a man through in such affairs. As a politician he has also had a very high reputation; he is perhaps the one orator the Colony possesses. As a debater he takes almost the highest position, his only rival being Mr. Merriman, and a contest between them is worth witnessing; both are skilful, and both are courteous, using their rapiers with the address and politeness of practised fencers, never giving a foul thrust or forgetting the gentlemanly politician. They have one point in common at all events—they both hate music, and this ought to make them "fit for treasons, stratagems and spoils"; but as I have never seen either of them manifest any inclination in that direction, I suppose I must consider that Shakespeare for once is wrong. I omitted to mention that Sir Thomas has also been Premier of this Colony.

As I have already in another chapter spoken of Mr. J. Rose-Innes, Q.C., and Mr. W. P. Shreiner, Q.C., there is no need for me to mention them here.

Then there is the Hon. H. H. Juta, Q.C., who was for a time Attorney-General of the Colony, and has now been elected the new Speaker of the House of Assembly. If an imposing appearance, a clear and distinct voice, unfailing courtesy to men of all parties, complete command of temper, and a wide acquaintance with the law and practice of Parliament, can fit him for the office, he ought to make, as I believe he will, an excellent Speaker. I suppose, however, he will have to resign his practice at the Bar, partially or entirely. This will be a pecuniary loss to him; but, fortunately, in his case not of much consequence. He has written an admirable translation of Grotius' "Introduction"; a difficult task, the original being written—as a late judge told me—in somewhat crabbed old Dutch.

Mr. Benjamin deserves mention as a man with excellent practice, and becoming a great authority in mercantile cases, especially on the law of sales, thus emulating his great namesake in England, now deceased.

Mr. Searle, Q.C., has more than once had the honour of being legal adviser to the High Commissioner of the Colony, and he sat for some time as Judge in the Eastern Districts Court during the absence of one of the occupants of the Bench. As lawyer and advocate he has deservedly gained a high reputation.

Mr. T. L. Graham is distinguished for his success in criminal defences, and has had probably a larger number of rascals among his clients than any other man of his standing at the Bar. His general practice is also good and well deserved.

Mr. Shiel has made his mark, and will, I think, make a still stronger one in the future. He has delivered law lectures, which are highly praised by those who have attended them.

Turning to the Court of the Eastern Districts, there is the Solicitor-General, Mr. Maasdorp, a brother of the Judge; Mr. Lardner Burke, a genial and much-liked practitioner; Mr. Tamplin, the tallest man in the profession, and equally at home in law, politics, or as Major commanding his Grahamstown Volunteers; and there is Mr. H. F. Blaine, whose success in the Court in which he practises and the Circuit to which he is attached, should have entitled him—I think long ere this—to be made a Q.C..

Then, looking to the High Court of Griqualand, there is Mr. Richard Solomon, Q.C., a man of whose merits it is difficult to speak too highly. He is a wrangler of Cambridge, and took a great many other honours at his University. No better lawyer exists. He is especially fluent in speech—for I believe he can cram more words into a minute than any other man I ever knew—but his words are always well worth listening to, for they are learned and logical. He has more than once had the offer of a judgeship, but his practice is too good to let him accept one. As a gentleman as well as a lawyer he is highly valued by all who know him.

Practising at the same Bar is Mr. Ward, who has much distinguished himself, and is daily rising in favour with the profession and the public.

And now I have to beg the forgiveness of those members of the three Bars whose names I have passed over, assuring them that I have done so, not from any want of appreciation of their merits, but from want of space.

On the whole, then, I think that the Colony has reason to be proud of its Bench and its Bar. As regards the Bench, no whisper of corruption, favouritism, or want of the highest sense of justice has ever been heard against any one of the judges. They have maintained the high character and prestige which have made the Bench of England the model one of the whole world. And the Bar also, in the person of every one of its members, has shown the fearless independence, the earnestness, and the sense of justice and duty which raise them to the level of their brethren in the profession at home.

And with these words I now bid farewell to Bench and Bar alike—and to my readers.